# GARFIELD'S
## GUIDE TO DIGITAL CITIZENSHIP

# A GARFIELD® GUIDE TO POSTING ONLINE
## Pause Before You Post

Garfield created by
JIM DAVIS

Written by
**Scott Nickel, Pat Craven, and Ciera Lovitt**

Illustrated by
**Glenn Zimmerman, Jeff Wesley, Lynette Nuding, and Larry Fentz**

Lerner Publications ◆ Minneapolis

This series will help you learn to stay safe and secure online, from playing games to downloading content from the internet. Use the resources and activities in the back of this book to learn more about cybersafety.

This content was created in partnership with the Center for Cyber Safety and Education. The Center for Cyber Safety and Education works to ensure that people across the globe have a positive and safe experience online through their educational programs, scholarships, and research. To learn more, visit www.IAmCyberSafe.org.

Illustrated by Lynette Nuding & Glenn Zimmerman
Written by Scott Nickel, Pat Craven, and Ciera Lovitt
Layouts by Jeff Wesley, Brad Hill, and Tom Howard
Cover pencils by Jeff Wesley
Cover inks & Colors by Larry Fentz

Visit Garfield online at https://www.garfield.com

Lerner Publications Company
An imprint of Lerner Publishing Group, Inc.
241 First Avenue North
Minneapolis, MN 55401 USA

For reading levels and more information, look up this title at www.lernerbooks.com.

Main text font provided by Garfield®.

**Library of Congress Cataloging-in-Publication Data**

Names: Nickel, Scott, author.
Title: A Garfield guide to posting online : pause before you post / Scott Nickel [and four others].
Description: Minneapolis : Lerner Publications, [2020] | Series: Garfield's guide to digital citizenship | Includes bibliographical references and index. | Audience: Ages 7–11. | Audience: K to Grade 3. | Summary: "Nermal loves posting on social media. But Arlene and Garfield think Nermal is sharing too much personal information. Online security expert Dr. Cybrina helps Nermal learn how much is too much to share online"— Provided by publisher.
Identifiers: LCCN 2019021158 (print) | LCCN 2019980899 (ebook) | ISBN 9781541587502 (paperback) | ISBN 9781541572799 (library binding) | ISBN 9781541583023 (pdf)
Subjects: LCSH: Garfield (Fictitious character) | Internet and children—Juvenile literature. | Internet—Security measures—Juvenile literature. | Online social networks—Safety measures—Juvenile literature.
Classification: LCC HQ784.I58 N533 2020 (print) | LCC HQ784.I58 (ebook) | DDC 004.67/8083—dc23

LC record available at https://lccn.loc.gov/2019021158
LC ebook record available at https://lccn.loc.gov/2019980899

Manufactured in the United States of America
1-46546-47591-8/13/2019

# PAUSE BEFORE YOU POST!

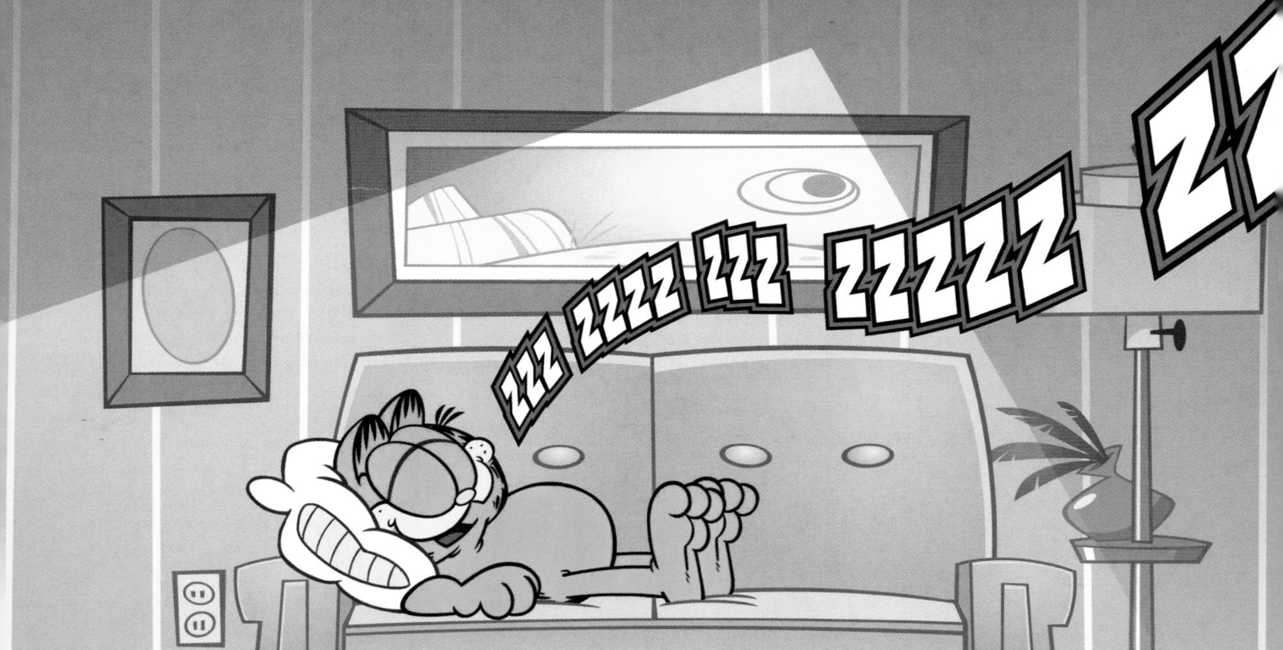
ZZZ ZZZZ ZZZ ZZZZZ

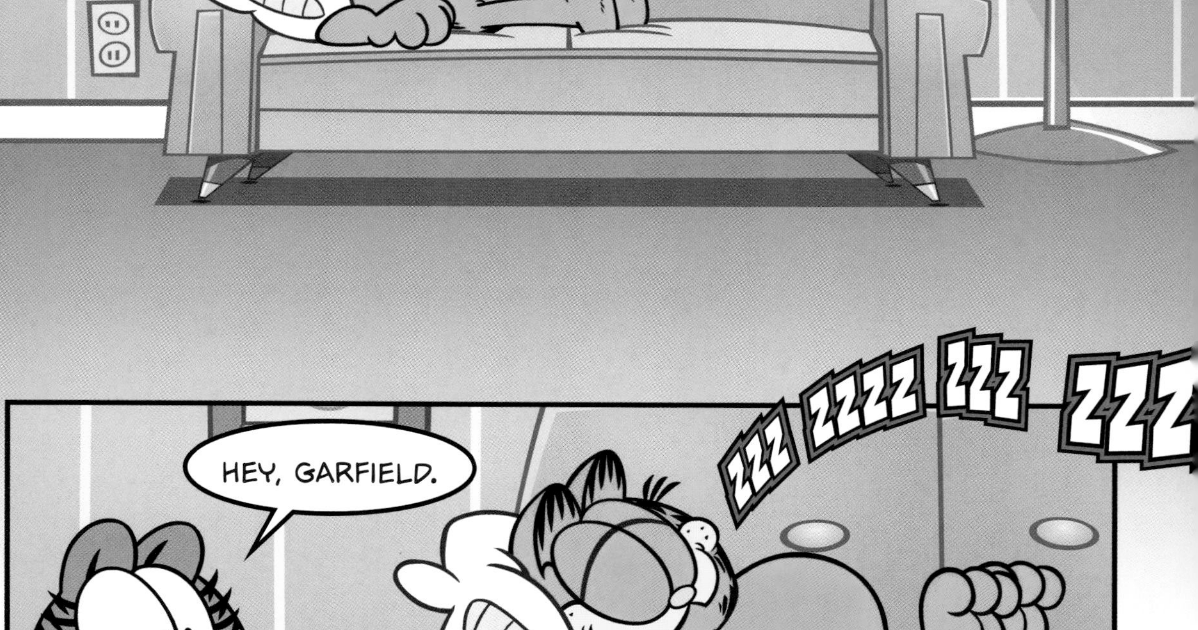
HEY, GARFIELD.
ZZZ ZZZZ ZZZ

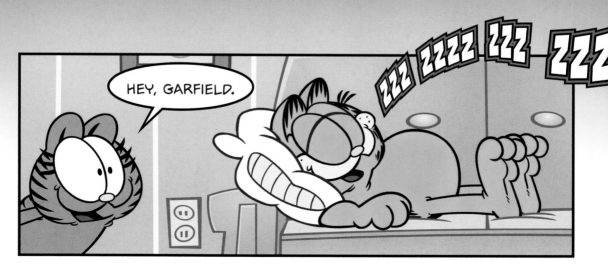

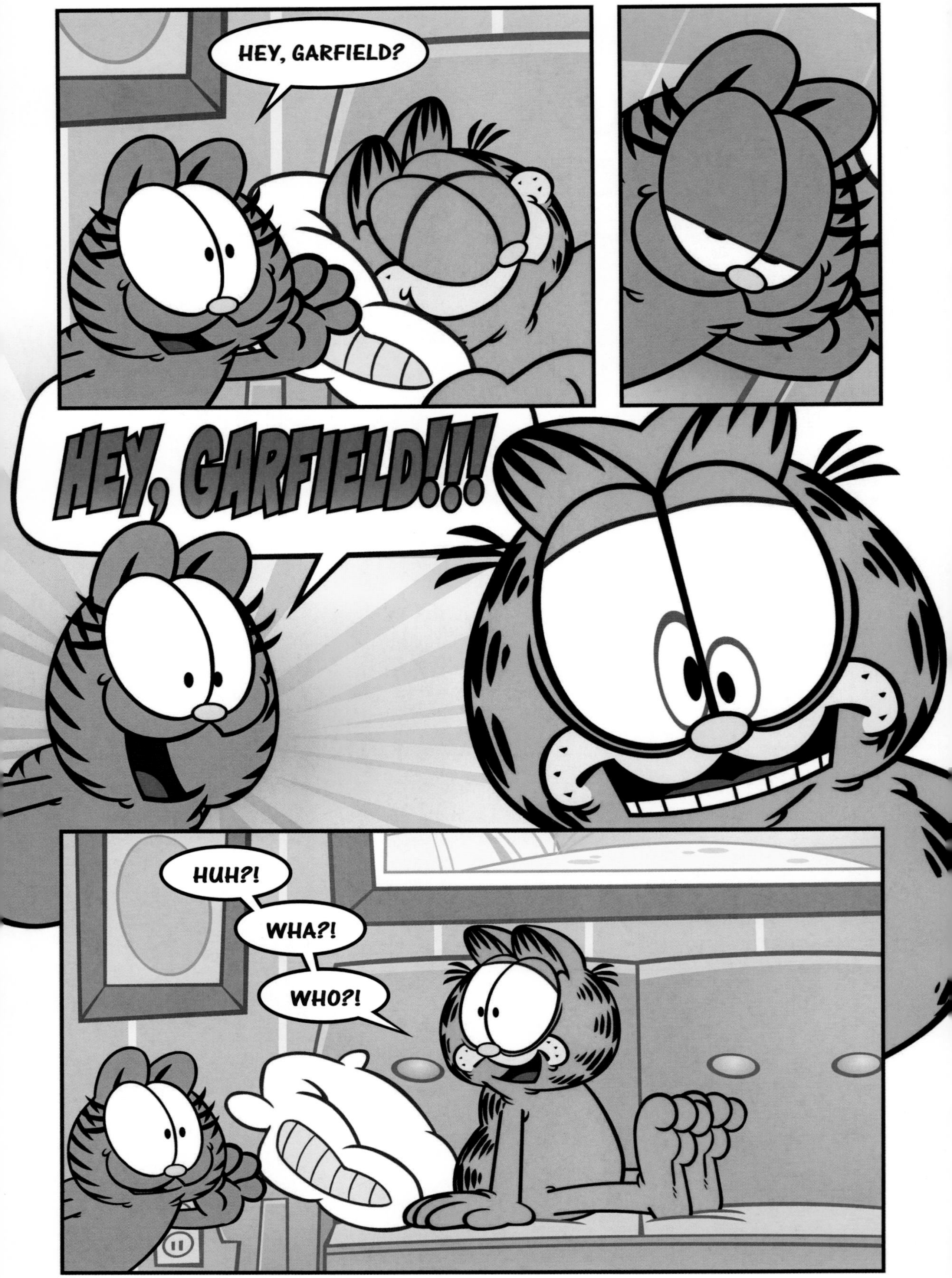
HEY, GARFIELD?
HEY, GARFIELD!!!
HUH?!
WHA?!
WHO?!

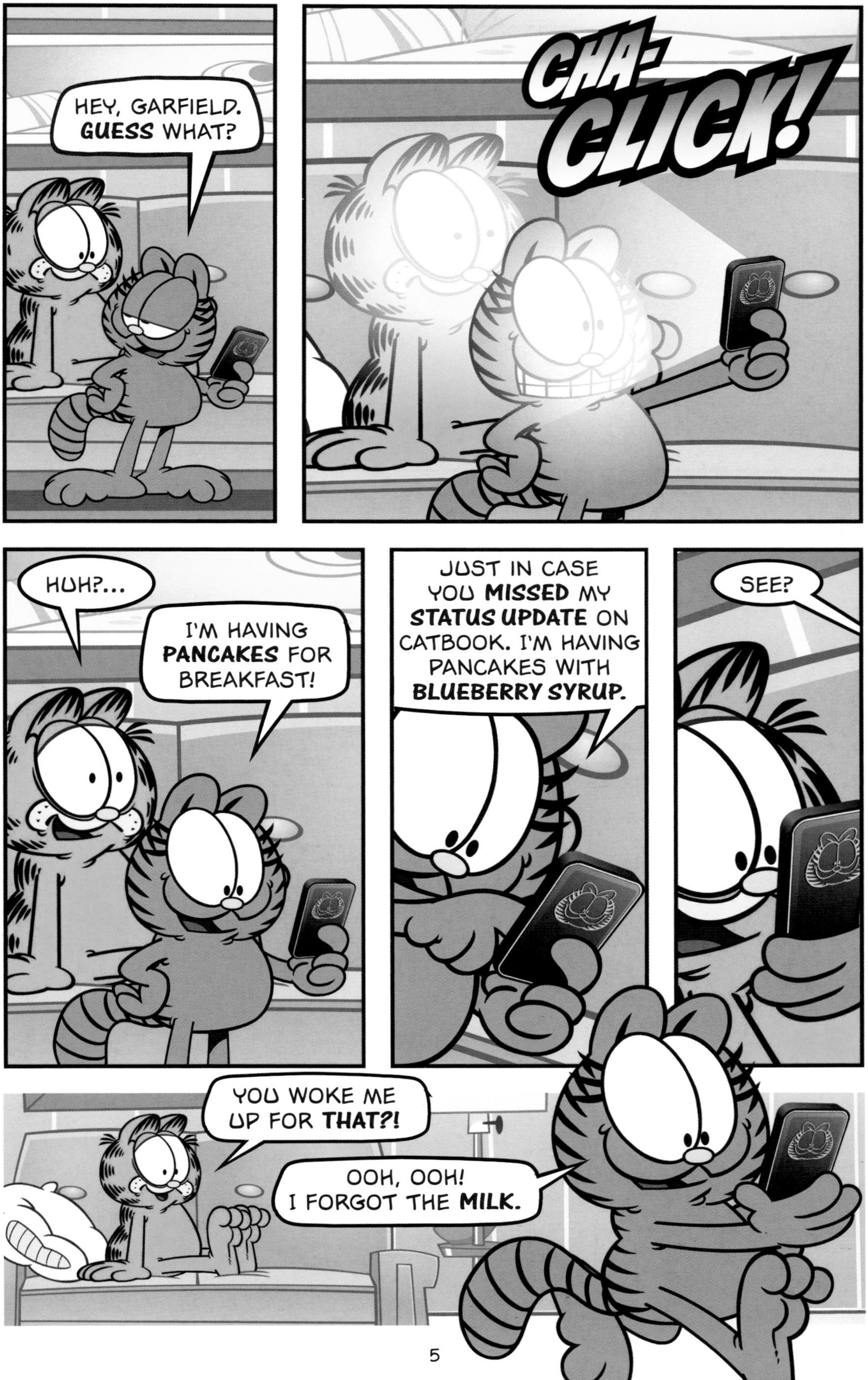

HEY, GARFIELD. GUESS WHAT?
CHA-CLICK!
HUH?...
I'M HAVING PANCAKES FOR BREAKFAST!
JUST IN CASE YOU MISSED MY STATUS UPDATE ON CATBOOK. I'M HAVING PANCAKES WITH BLUEBERRY SYRUP.
SEE?
YOU WOKE ME UP FOR THAT?!
OOH, OOH! I FORGOT THE MILK.

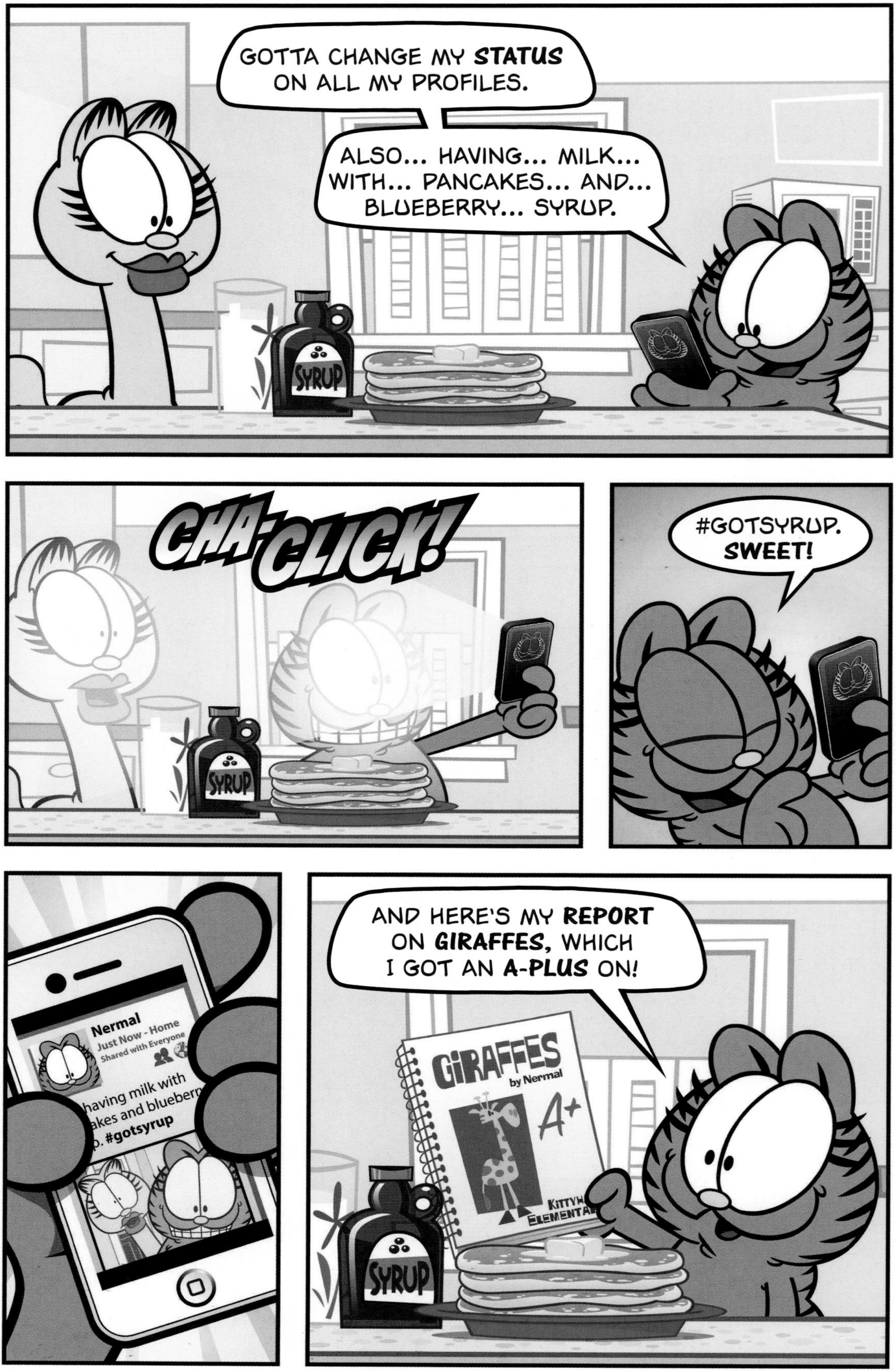
GOTTA CHANGE MY **STATUS** ON ALL MY PROFILES.
ALSO... HAVING... MILK... WITH... PANCAKES... AND... BLUEBERRY... SYRUP.
SYRUP
CHA-CLICK!
SYRUP
#GOTSYRUP. **SWEET!**
Nermal
Just Now - Home
Shared with Everyone
having milk with
#gotsyrup
AND HERE'S MY **REPORT** ON **GIRAFFES,** WHICH I GOT AN **A-PLUS** ON!
GIRAFFES
by Nermal
A+
SYRUP

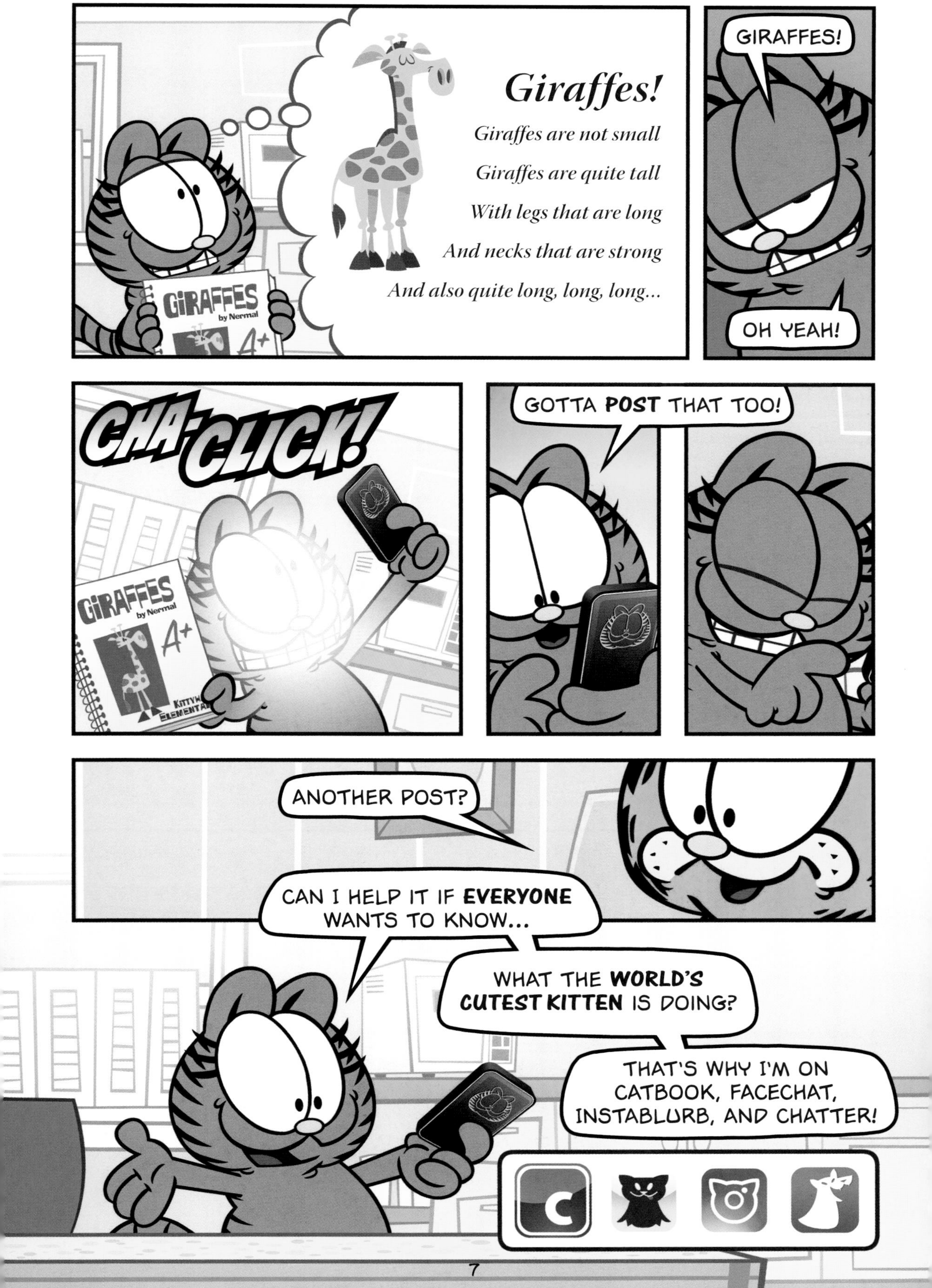
Giraffes!
Giraffes are not small
Giraffes are quite tall
With legs that are long
And necks that are strong
And also quite long, long, long...
GIRAFFES by Nermal A+
GIRAFFES!
OH YEAH!
CHA-CLICK!
GOTTA POST THAT TOO!
ANOTHER POST?
CAN I HELP IT IF EVERYONE WANTS TO KNOW...
WHAT THE WORLD'S CUTEST KITTEN IS DOING?
THAT'S WHY I'M ON CATBOOK, FACECHAT, INSTABLURB, AND CHATTER!

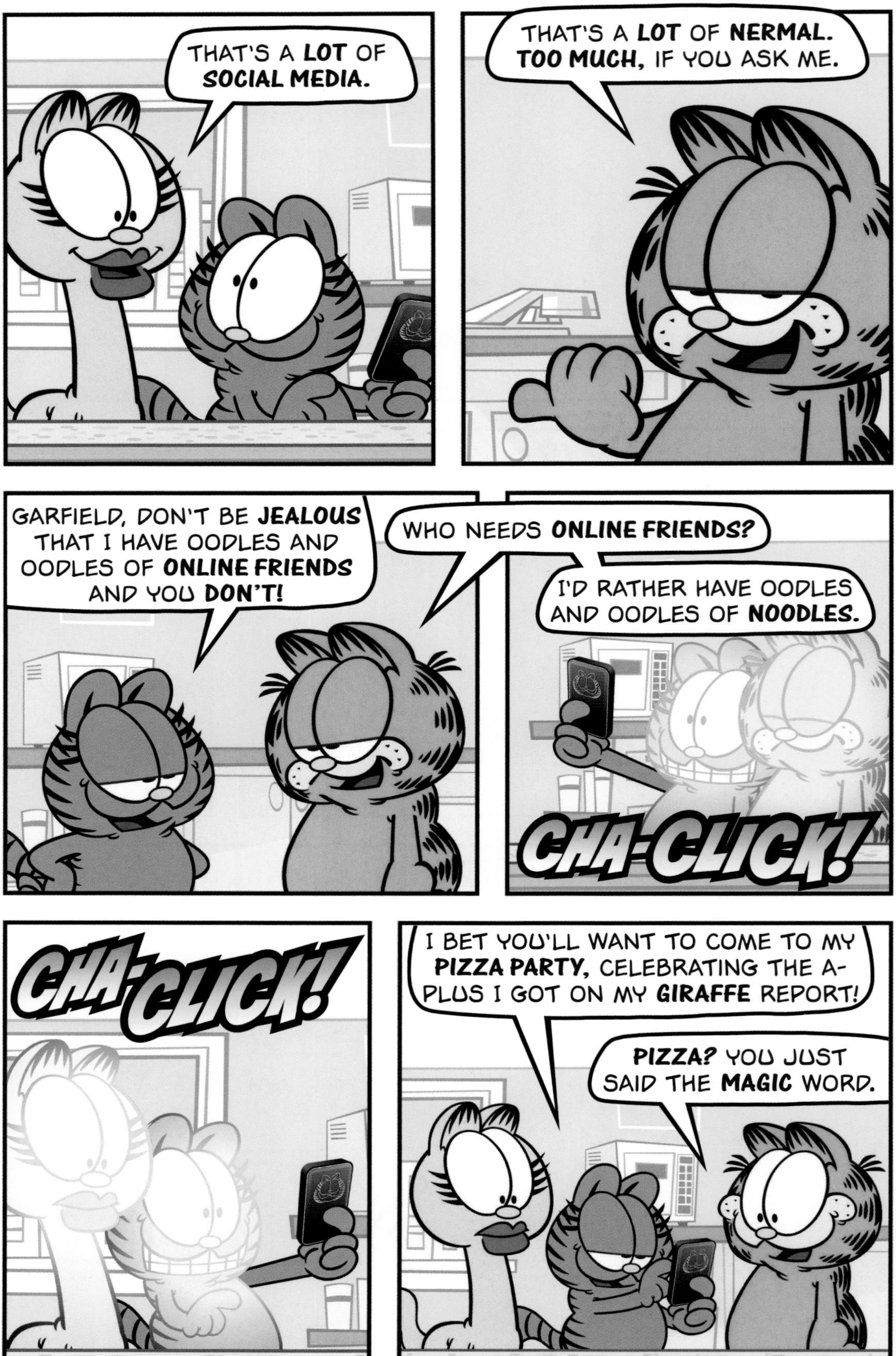
THAT'S A LOT OF SOCIAL MEDIA.
THAT'S A LOT OF NERMAL. TOO MUCH, IF YOU ASK ME.
GARFIELD, DON'T BE JEALOUS THAT I HAVE OODLES AND OODLES OF ONLINE FRIENDS AND YOU DON'T!
WHO NEEDS ONLINE FRIENDS?
I'D RATHER HAVE OODLES AND OODLES OF NOODLES.
CHA-CLICK!
CHA-CLICK!
I BET YOU'LL WANT TO COME TO MY PIZZA PARTY, CELEBRATING THE A-PLUS I GOT ON MY GIRAFFE REPORT!
PIZZA? YOU JUST SAID THE MAGIC WORD.

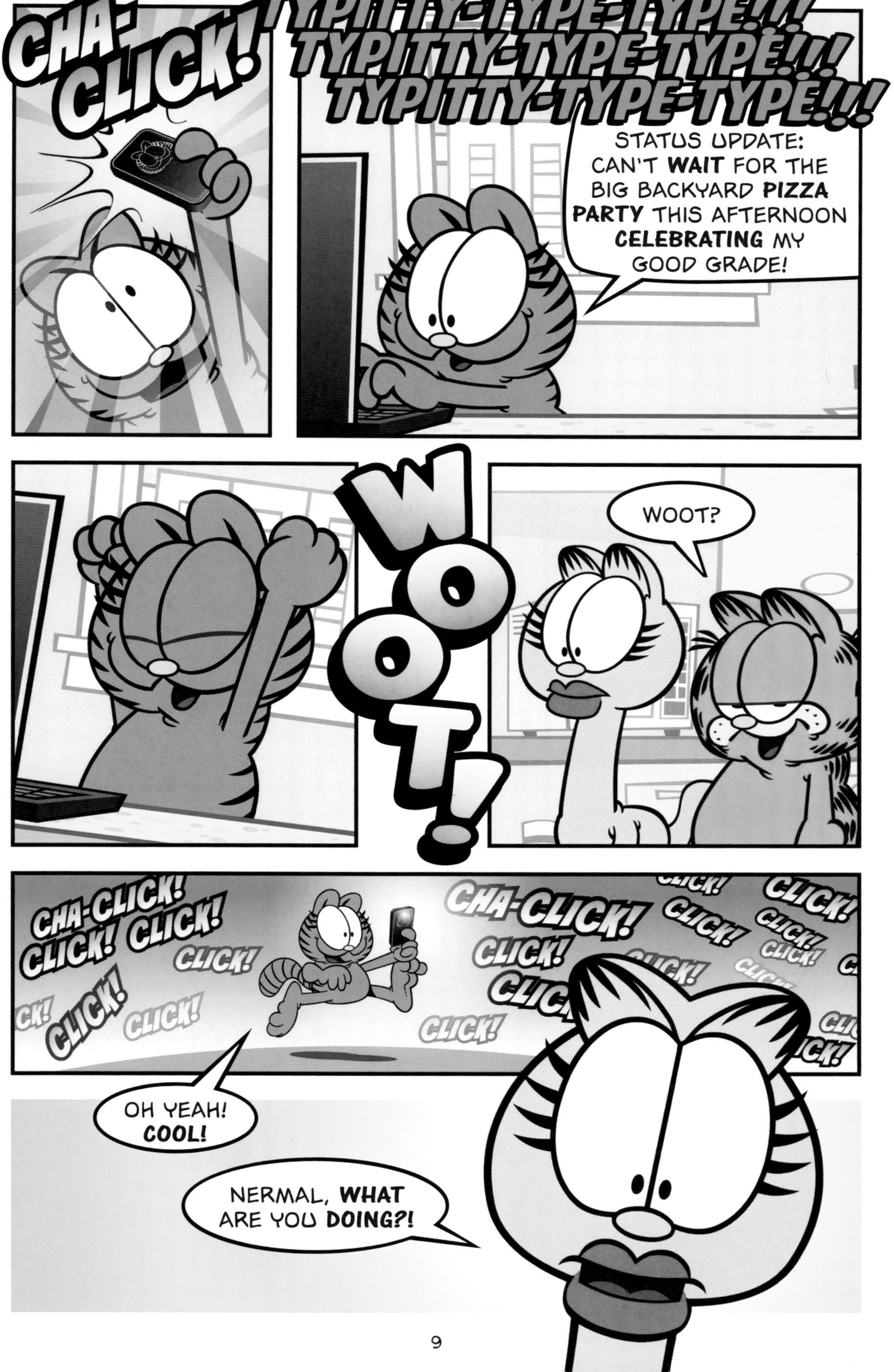

CHA-CLICK!
TYPITTY-TYPE-TYPE!!!
TYPITTY-TYPE-TYPE!!!
TYPITTY-TYPE-TYPE!!!
STATUS UPDATE: CAN'T WAIT FOR THE BIG BACKYARD PIZZA PARTY THIS AFTERNOON CELEBRATING MY GOOD GRADE!
WOOT!
WOOT?
CHA-CLICK! CLICK! CLICK!
CLICK!
CLICK!
CLICK!
CHA-CLICK!
CLICK!
CLICK!
CLICK!
OH YEAH! COOL!
NERMAL, WHAT ARE YOU DOING?!

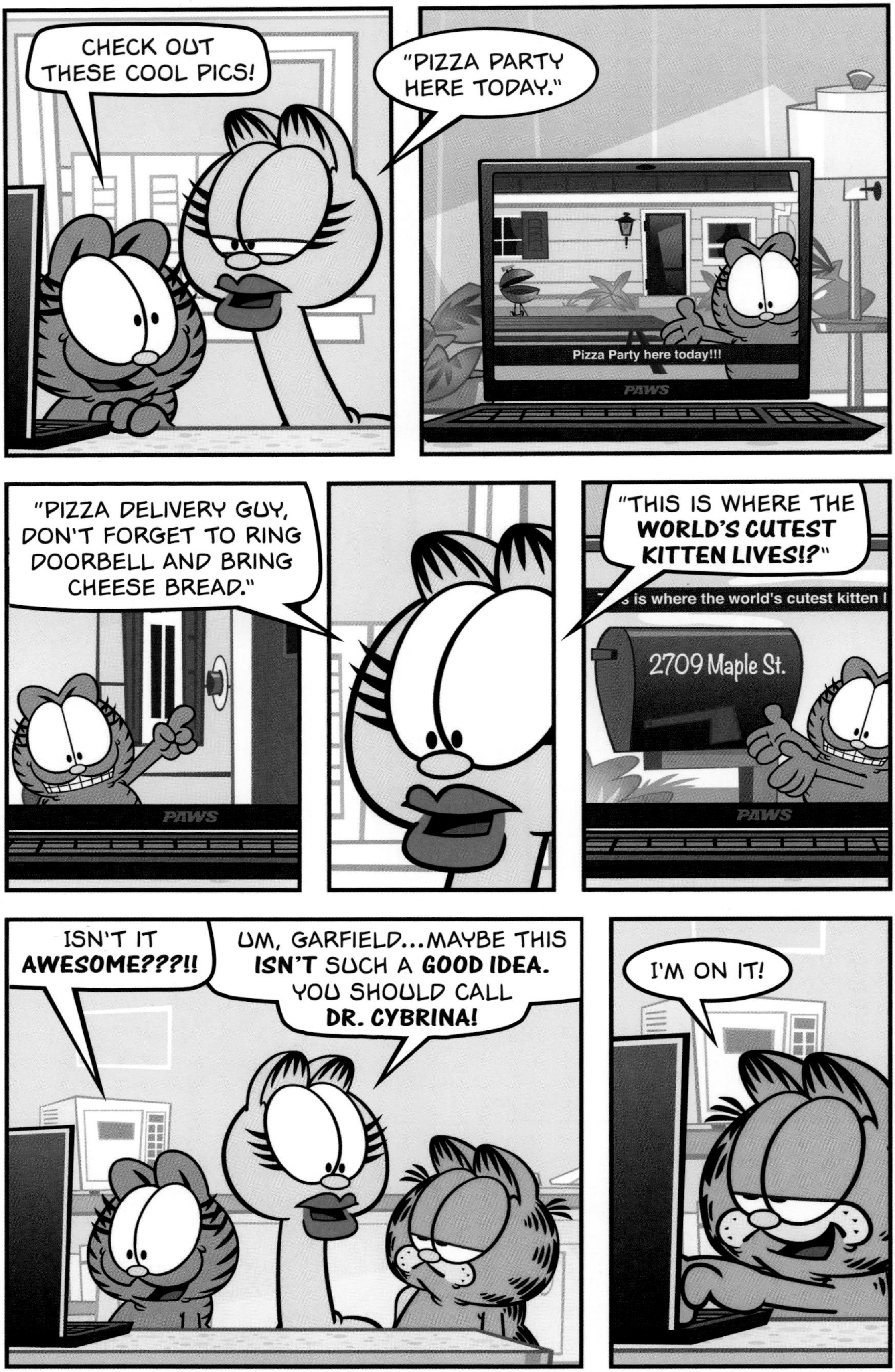
CHECK OUT THESE COOL PICS!
"PIZZA PARTY HERE TODAY."
Pizza Party here today!!!
PAWS
"PIZZA DELIVERY GUY, DON'T FORGET TO RING DOORBELL AND BRING CHEESE BREAD."
PAWS
"THIS IS WHERE THE WORLD'S CUTEST KITTEN LIVES!?"
2709 Maple St.
PAWS
ISN'T IT AWESOME???!!
UM, GARFIELD...MAYBE THIS ISN'T SUCH A GOOD IDEA. YOU SHOULD CALL DR. CYBRINA!
I'M ON IT!

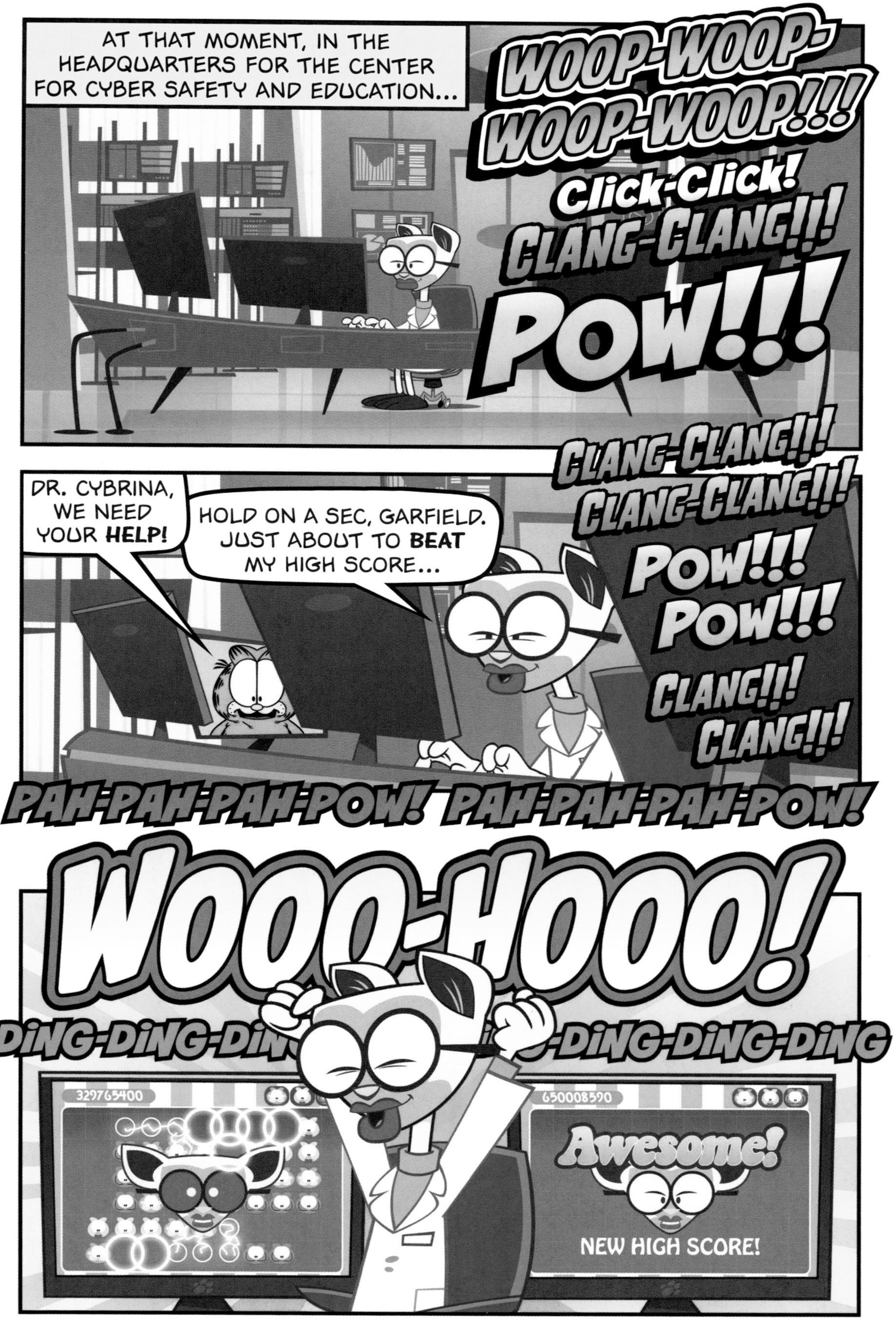
AT THAT MOMENT, IN THE HEADQUARTERS FOR THE CENTER FOR CYBER SAFETY AND EDUCATION...
WOOP-WOOP-WOOP-WOOP!!!
Click-Click!
CLANG-CLANG!!!
POW!!!
CLANG-CLANG!!!
CLANG-CLANG!!!
DR. CYBRINA, WE NEED YOUR **HELP**!
HOLD ON A SEC, GARFIELD. JUST ABOUT TO **BEAT** MY HIGH SCORE...
POW!!!
POW!!!
CLANG!!!
CLANG!!!
PAH-PAH-PAH-POW! PAH-PAH-PAH-POW!
WOOO-HOOOO!
DiNG-DiNG-DiN
-DiNG-DiNG-DiNG
329765400
650008590
Awesome!
NEW HIGH SCORE!

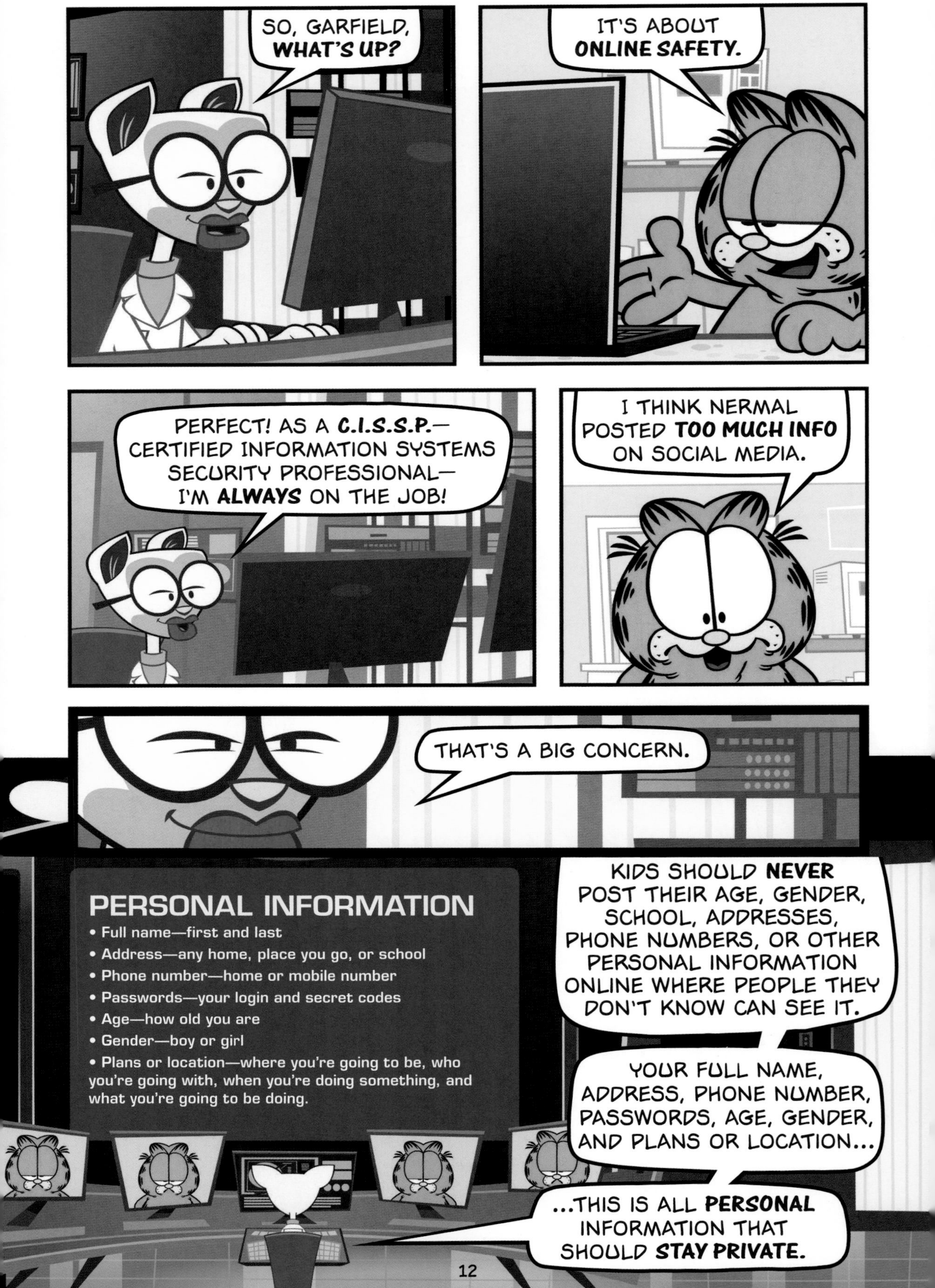
SO, GARFIELD, WHAT'S UP?
IT'S ABOUT ONLINE SAFETY.
PERFECT! AS A C.I.S.S.P.—CERTIFIED INFORMATION SYSTEMS SECURITY PROFESSIONAL—I'M ALWAYS ON THE JOB!
I THINK NERMAL POSTED TOO MUCH INFO ON SOCIAL MEDIA.
THAT'S A BIG CONCERN.
PERSONAL INFORMATION
• Full name—first and last
• Address—any home, place you go, or school
• Phone number—home or mobile number
• Passwords—your login and secret codes
• Age—how old you are
• Gender—boy or girl
• Plans or location—where you're going to be, who you're going with, when you're doing something, and what you're going to be doing.
KIDS SHOULD NEVER POST THEIR AGE, GENDER, SCHOOL, ADDRESSES, PHONE NUMBERS, OR OTHER PERSONAL INFORMATION ONLINE WHERE PEOPLE THEY DON'T KNOW CAN SEE IT.
YOUR FULL NAME, ADDRESS, PHONE NUMBER, PASSWORDS, AGE, GENDER, AND PLANS OR LOCATION...
...THIS IS ALL PERSONAL INFORMATION THAT SHOULD STAY PRIVATE.

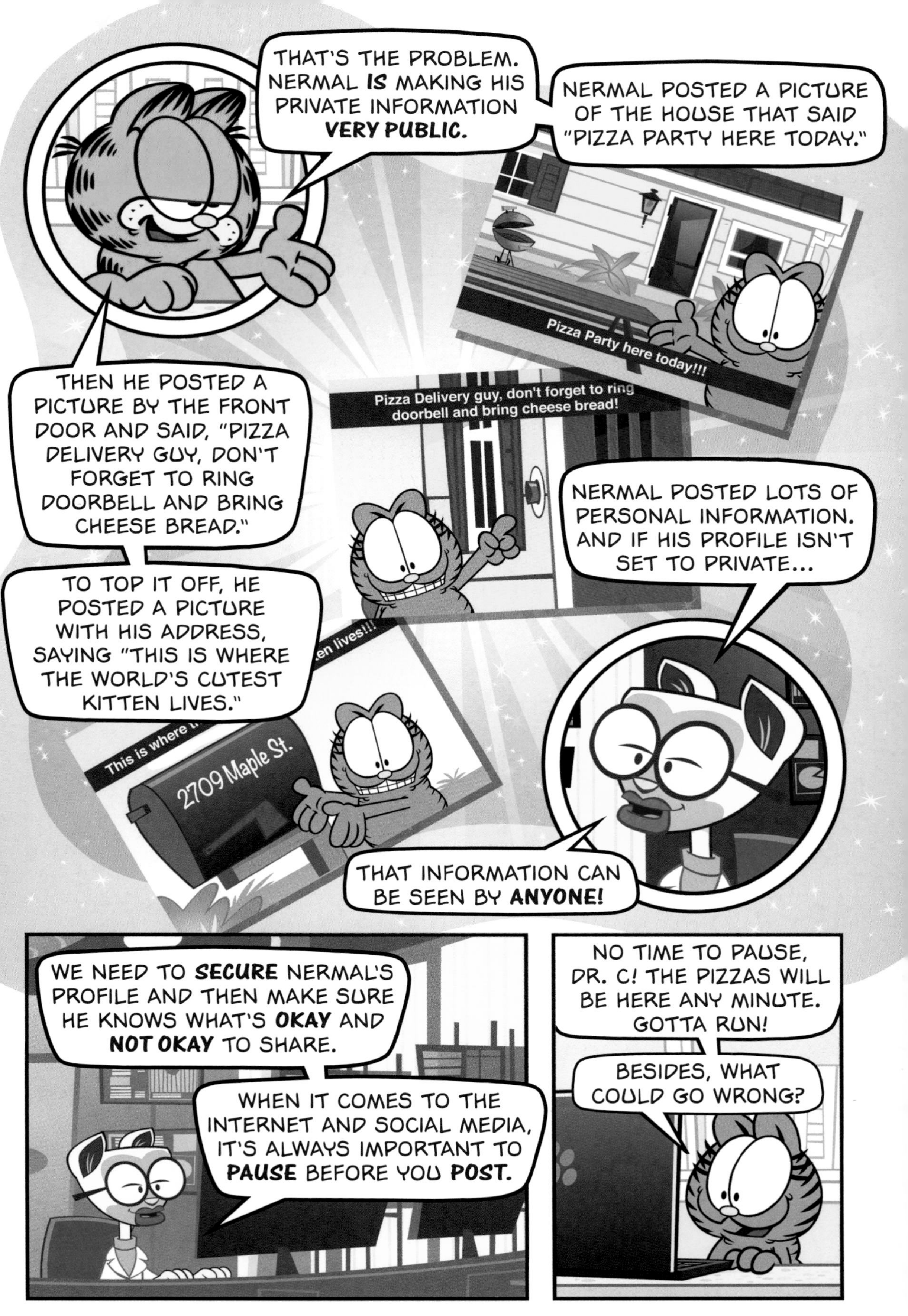

THAT'S THE PROBLEM. NERMAL **IS** MAKING HIS PRIVATE INFORMATION **VERY PUBLIC.**
NERMAL POSTED A PICTURE OF THE HOUSE THAT SAID "PIZZA PARTY HERE TODAY."
Pizza Party here today!!!
THEN HE POSTED A PICTURE BY THE FRONT DOOR AND SAID, "PIZZA DELIVERY GUY, DON'T FORGET TO RING DOORBELL AND BRING CHEESE BREAD."
Pizza Delivery guy, don't forget to ring doorbell and bring cheese bread!
NERMAL POSTED LOTS OF PERSONAL INFORMATION. AND IF HIS PROFILE ISN'T SET TO PRIVATE...
TO TOP IT OFF, HE POSTED A PICTURE WITH HIS ADDRESS, SAYING "THIS IS WHERE THE WORLD'S CUTEST KITTEN LIVES."
This is where
en lives!!!
2709 Maple St.
THAT INFORMATION CAN BE SEEN BY **ANYONE!**
WE NEED TO **SECURE** NERMAL'S PROFILE AND THEN MAKE SURE HE KNOWS WHAT'S **OKAY** AND **NOT OKAY** TO SHARE.
WHEN IT COMES TO THE INTERNET AND SOCIAL MEDIA, IT'S ALWAYS IMPORTANT TO **PAUSE** BEFORE YOU **POST.**
NO TIME TO PAUSE, DR. C! THE PIZZAS WILL BE HERE ANY MINUTE. GOTTA RUN!
BESIDES, WHAT COULD GO WRONG?

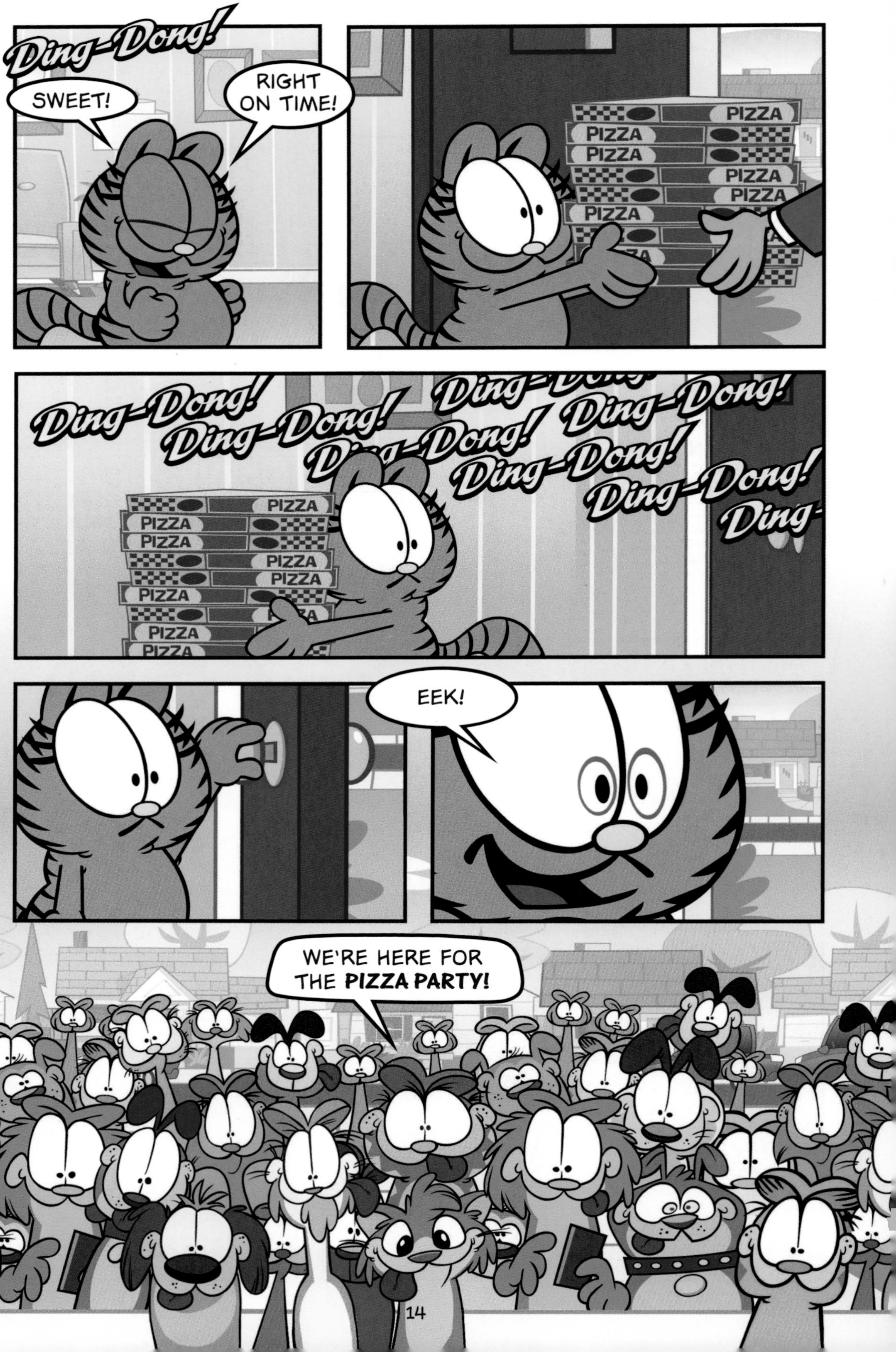

Ding-Dong!
SWEET!
RIGHT ON TIME!
PIZZA
Ding-Dong!
Ding-Dong!
Ding-Dong!
Ding-Dong!
Ding-Dong!
Ding-Dong!
Ding-
EEK!
WE'RE HERE FOR THE **PIZZA PARTY!**

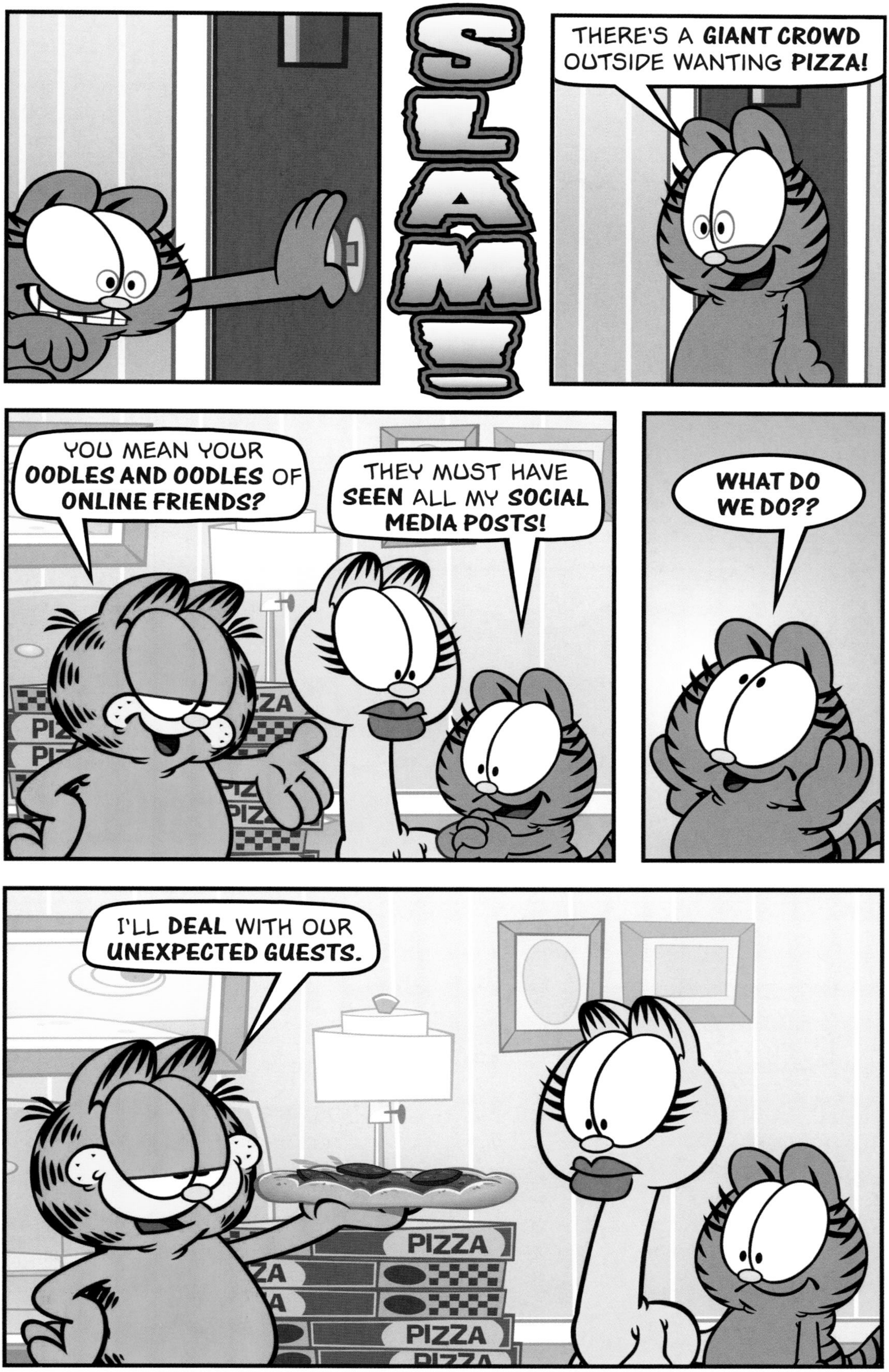

SLAM!
THERE'S A GIANT CROWD OUTSIDE WANTING PIZZA!
YOU MEAN YOUR OODLES AND OODLES OF ONLINE FRIENDS?
THEY MUST HAVE SEEN ALL MY SOCIAL MEDIA POSTS!
WHAT DO WE DO??
I'LL DEAL WITH OUR UNEXPECTED GUESTS.
PIZZA
PIZZA

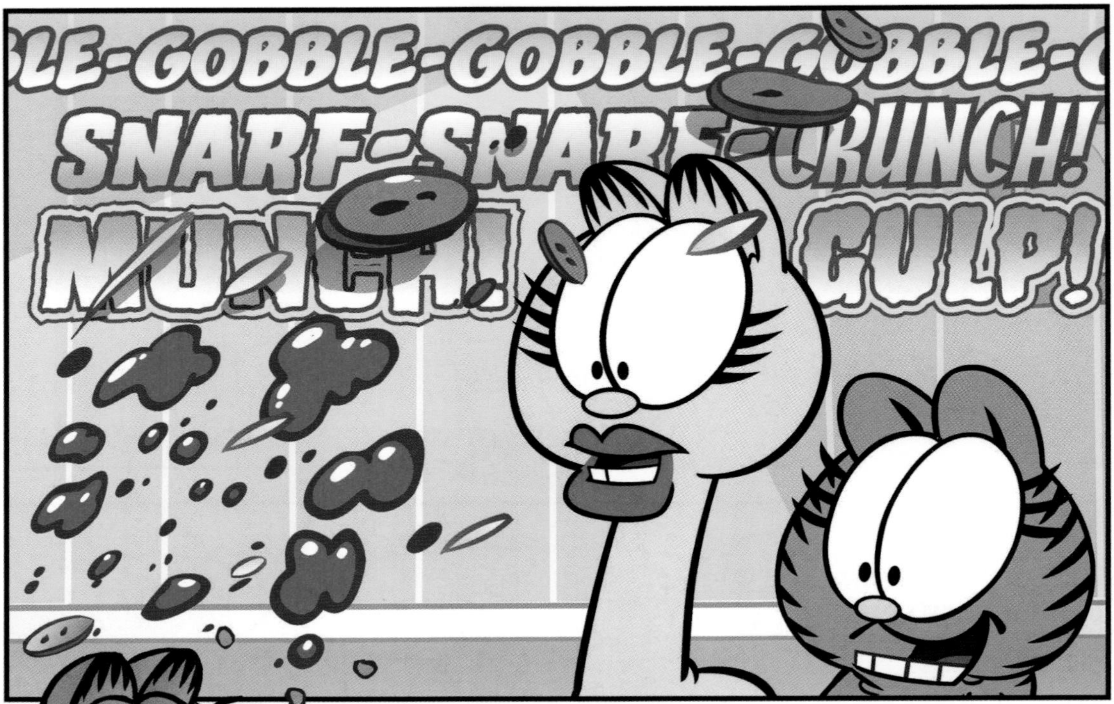

GOBBLE-GOBBLE-GOBBLE
SNARF-SNARF-CRUNCH!
MUNCH!
GULP!


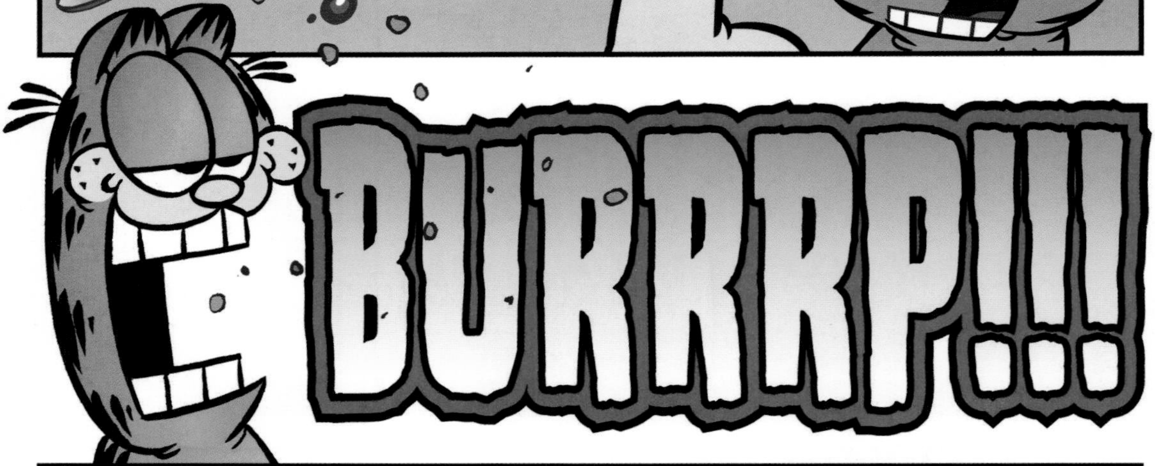

BURRRP!!!


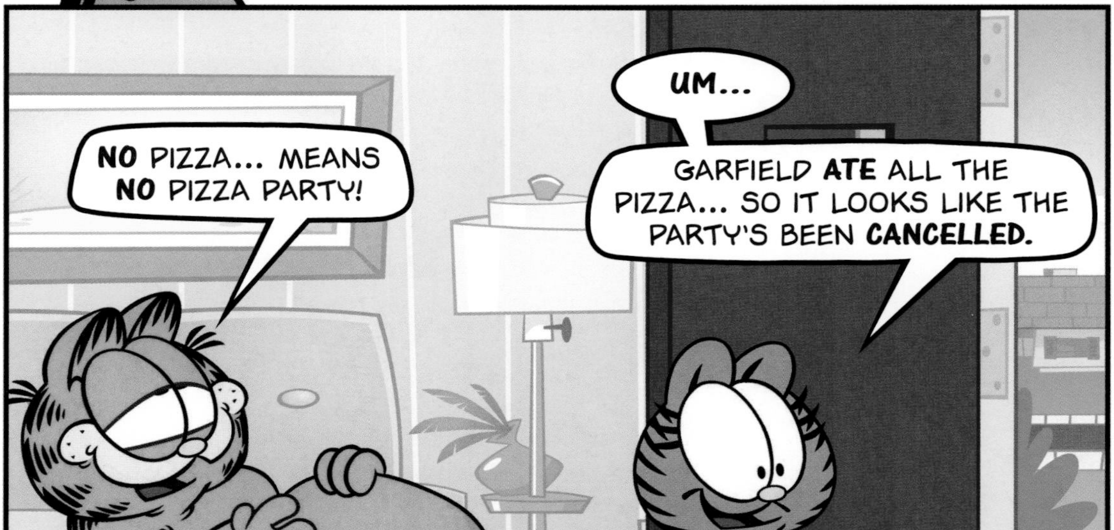

UM...
NO PIZZA... MEANS NO PIZZA PARTY!
GARFIELD ATE ALL THE PIZZA... SO IT LOOKS LIKE THE PARTY'S BEEN CANCELLED.

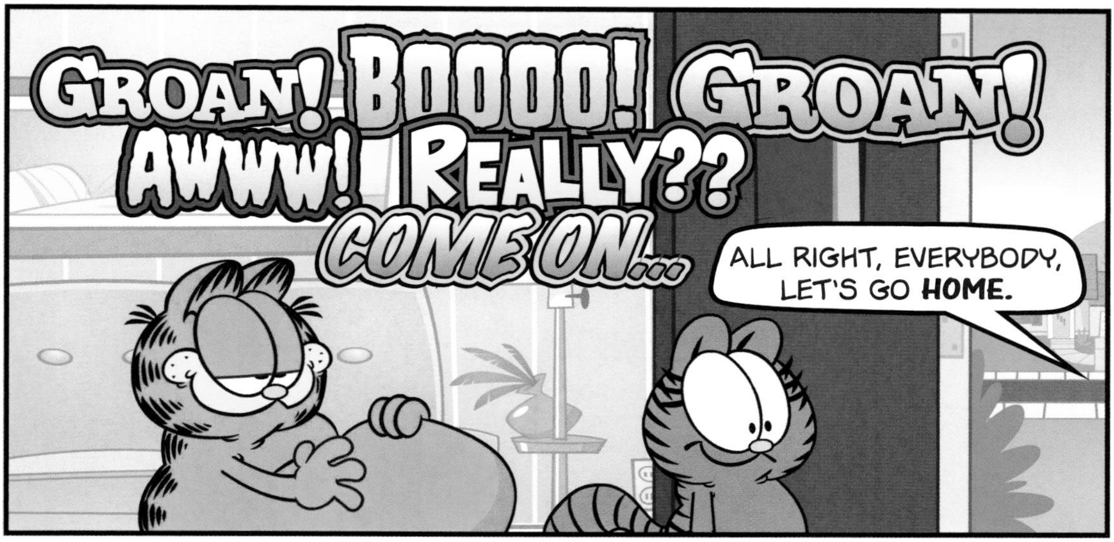
GROAN! BOOOO! GROAN!
AWWW! REALLY??
COME ON...
ALL RIGHT, EVERYBODY, LET'S GO **HOME.**

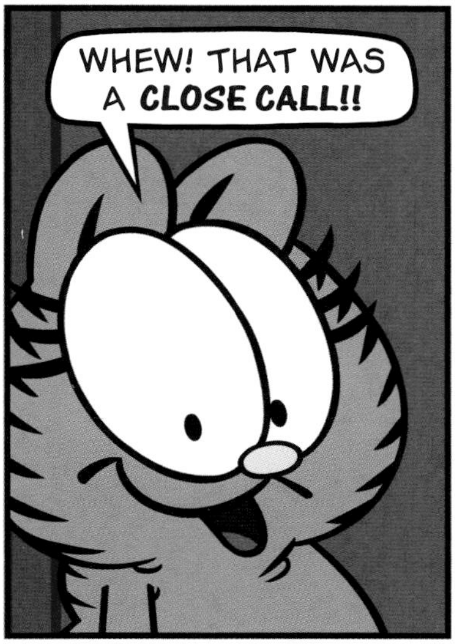
WHEW! THAT WAS A **CLOSE CALL!!**

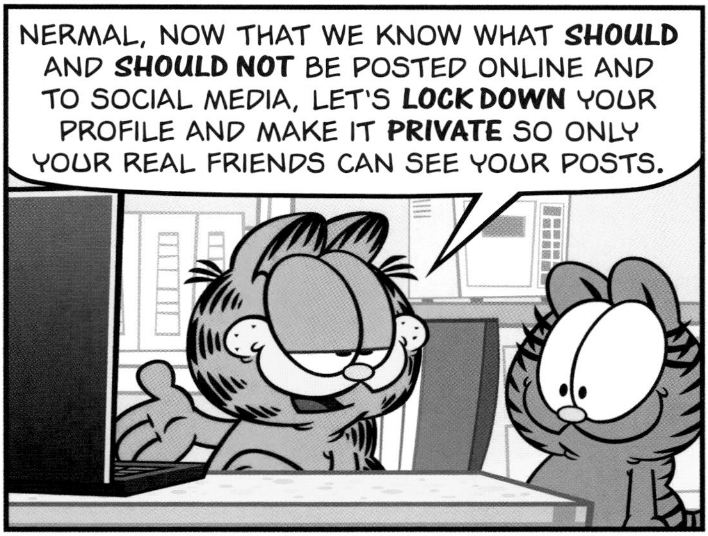
NERMAL, NOW THAT WE KNOW WHAT **SHOULD** AND **SHOULD NOT** BE POSTED ONLINE AND TO SOCIAL MEDIA, LET'S **LOCK DOWN** YOUR PROFILE AND MAKE IT **PRIVATE** SO ONLY YOUR REAL FRIENDS CAN SEE YOUR POSTS.

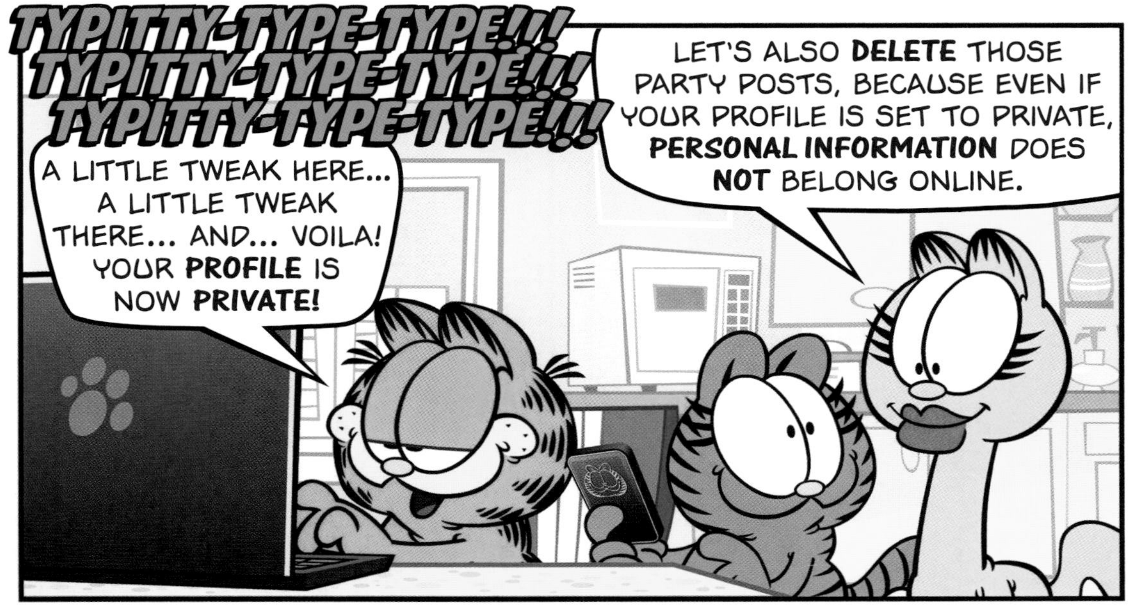
TYPITTY-TYPE-TYPE!!! TYPITTY-TYPE-TYPE!!! TYPITTY-TYPE-TYPE!!!
A LITTLE TWEAK HERE... A LITTLE TWEAK THERE... AND... VOILA! YOUR **PROFILE** IS NOW **PRIVATE!**
LET'S ALSO **DELETE** THOSE PARTY POSTS, BECAUSE EVEN IF YOUR PROFILE IS SET TO PRIVATE, **PERSONAL INFORMATION** DOES **NOT** BELONG ONLINE.

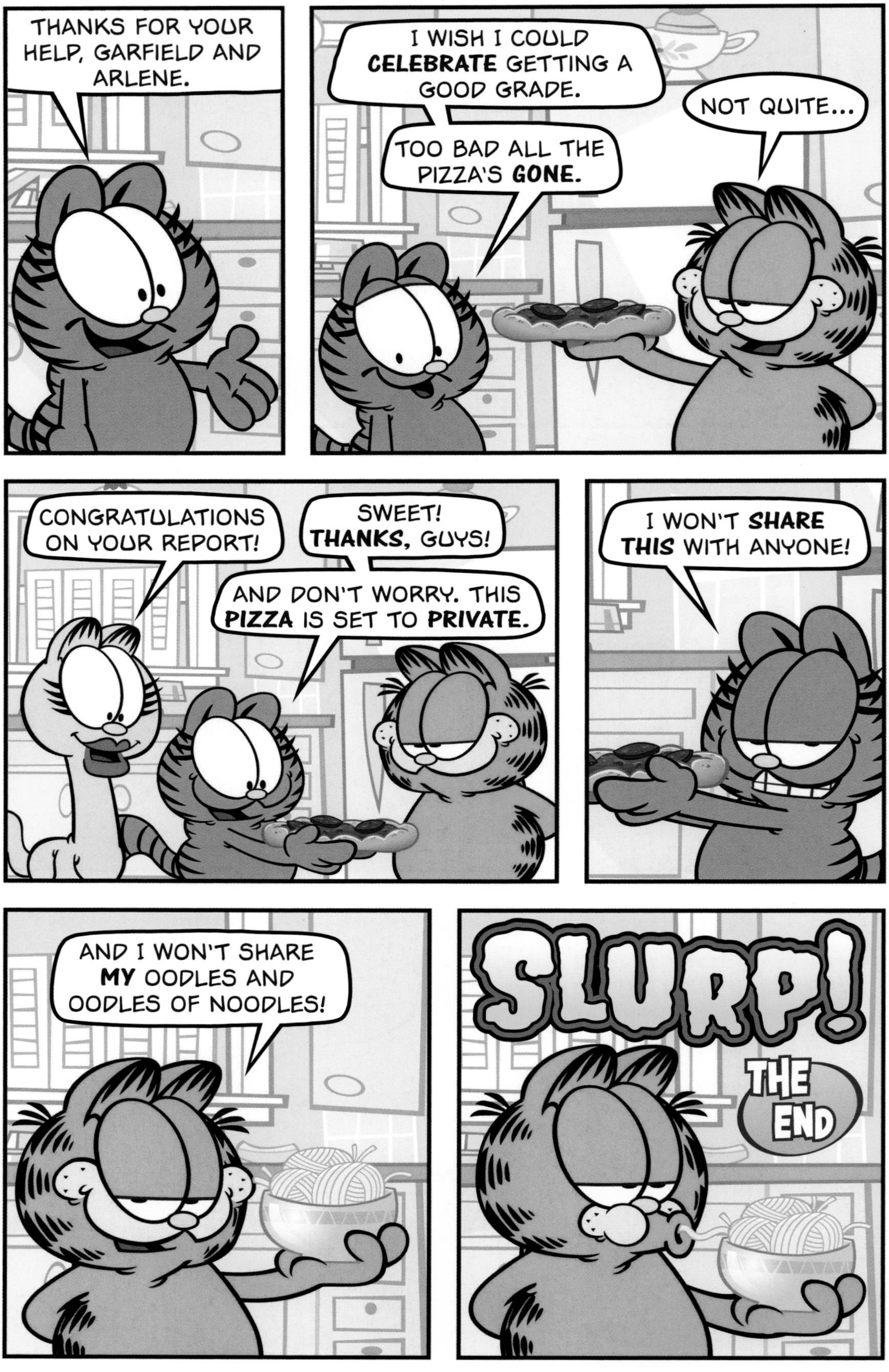
THANKS FOR YOUR HELP, GARFIELD AND ARLENE.
I WISH I COULD **CELEBRATE** GETTING A GOOD GRADE.
TOO BAD ALL THE PIZZA'S **GONE.**
NOT QUITE...
CONGRATULATIONS ON YOUR REPORT!
SWEET! **THANKS,** GUYS!
AND DON'T WORRY. THIS **PIZZA** IS SET TO **PRIVATE.**
I WON'T **SHARE THIS** WITH ANYONE!
AND I WON'T SHARE **MY** OODLES AND OODLES OF NOODLES!
SLURP!
THE END

# ACTIVITY: POSTING PERSONAL INFORMATION

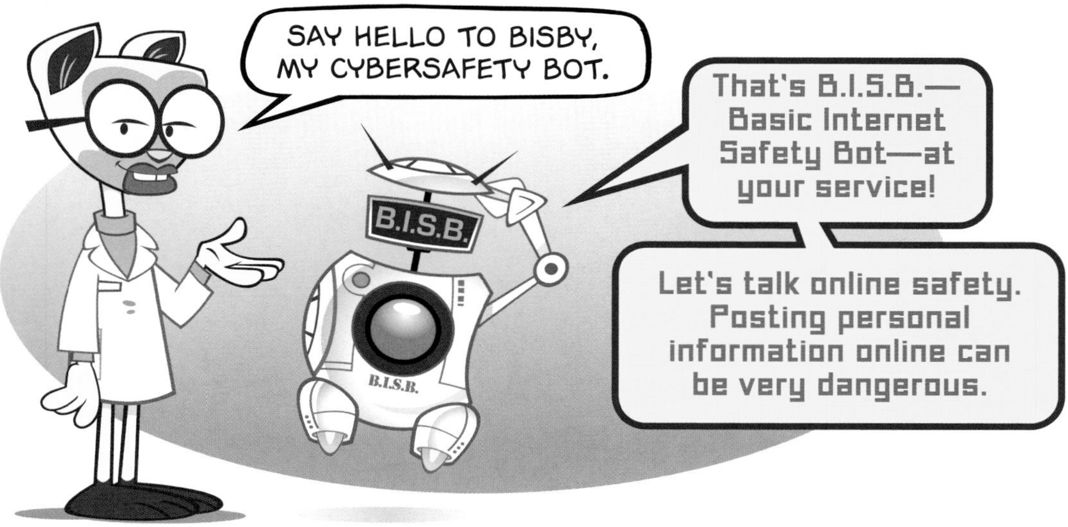
SAY HELLO TO BISBY, MY CYBERSAFETY BOT.
That's B.I.S.B.— Basic Internet Safety Bot—at your service!
Let's talk online safety. Posting personal information online can be very dangerous.
B.I.S.B.
B.I.S.B.

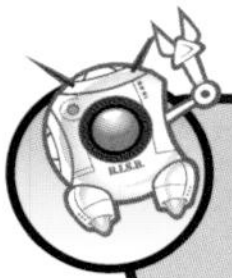

## PART 1: TRUE OR FALSE

ARE THESE STATEMENTS TRUE OR FALSE? WRITE YOUR ANSWERS ON A SEPARATE SHEET OF PAPER.

1. It's okay to post about your favorite music, movies, and sports teams.
2. It's okay to post your age or the year you were born.
3. It's okay to post your phone number and address so all of your online friends can call and visit.
4. It's okay to post vacation pictures while you are still on vacation.
5. It's okay to say that you're home alone if you think your profile has been set to private.
6. It's okay to post photos of your field trip after you get home.
7. It's okay to post about your accomplishments in sports and school.
8. It's always a good idea to get an adult to help you check your settings in social media to make sure that your profiles, posts, and pictures remain private.

9. **It's never okay to "friend" or "follow" strangers.**

10. **The more online friends that you have, the more popular you really are.**

11. **You should only "friend" or "follow" family and friends you already know.**

12. **Online friends are not the same as real friends.**

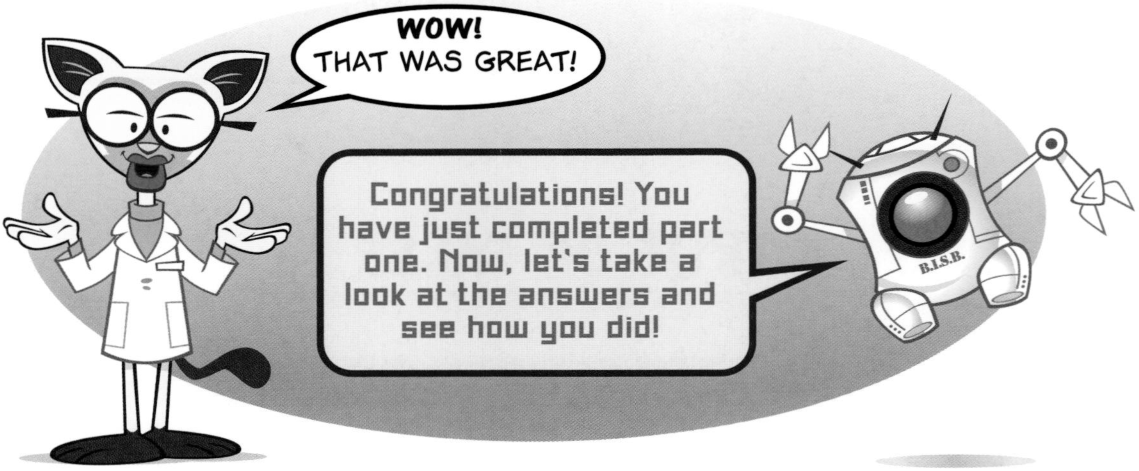
WOW!
THAT WAS GREAT!
Congratulations! You have just completed part one. Now, let's take a look at the answers and see how you did!
B.I.S.B.

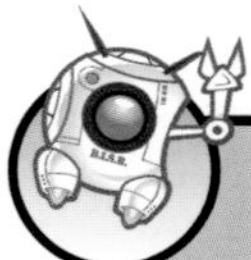

# PART 1: TRUE OR FALSE ANSWERS

POSTING PERSONAL INFORMATION ONLINE CAN BE VERY DANGEROUS. BELOW ARE THE CORRECT ANSWERS TO THE TRUE OR FALSE QUESTIONS.

1. **It's okay to post about your favorite music, movies, and sports teams.**

   True. Posting about your favorite music, movies, and sports teams is fine. Just be sure not to give away any personal information.

2. **It's okay to post your age or the year you were born.**

   False. Your age or the year you were born is personal information that you don't want to share with strangers.

3. **It's okay to post your phone number and address so all of your online friends can call and visit.**

   False. You don't want to post personal information like your phone number and address that can be shared with people you don't know.

4. **It's okay to post vacation pictures while you are still on vacation.**

   False. It may seem okay, but posting vacation pictures while you are on vacation tells strangers that your family isn't home. You don't want any bad people visiting your home while you are gone! Stay safe and secure, and don't post personal information.

5. **It's okay to say that you're home alone if you think your profile has been set to private.**

   False. Even if your profile is set to private, you don't want to post any information that tells people you are home alone.

6. **It's okay to post photos of your field trip after you get home.**

   True. You can post pictures after your trip, but you don't want to give out any information about where you are when you're not home.

7. **It's okay to post about your accomplishments in sports and school.**

   True. Sharing your achievements online is fun. Just don't give away any personal information.

8. **It's always a good idea to get an adult to help you check your settings in social media to make sure that your profiles, posts, and pictures remain private.**

   True. You don't want strangers or people that you don't know well looking at your posts. Keep all your settings private.

9. **It's never okay to "friend" or "follow" strangers.**

   True. If you don't know someone, you should never "friend" or "follow" them online.

10. **The more online friends that you have, the more popular you really are.**

    False. Online friends aren't the same as real friends. Having lots of online friends can be fun, but it doesn't really make you more popular.

**11. You should only "friend" or "follow" family and friends you already know.**

True. Never "friend" or "follow" someone that you don't really know.

**12. Online friends are not the same as real friends.**

True. It's fun to have friends, but knowing someone online isn't like knowing them in real life. People can make up names and information when they go online. Sometimes they may not even be who they say they are.

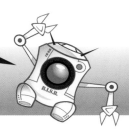

Excellent work. You're on your way to becoming a cybersafety superstar!
Now you are ready to help Nermal stay safe and secure online!
B.I.S.B.

# Part 2: What's Wrong with This Picture?

CHOOSE THE ANSWER THAT BEST DESCRIBES WHY NERMAL SHOULD NOT POST THESE PHOTOS ONLINE. WRITE YOUR ANSWERS ON A SEPARATE SHEET OF PAPER.

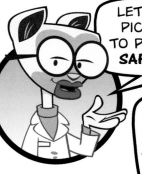

LET'S TAKE A LOOK AT THE PICTURES NERMAL WANTS TO POST AND HELP HIM STAY **SAFE** AND **SECURE** ONLINE.
NERMAL IS SO EXCITED ABOUT WHAT HE IS HAVING FOR BREAKFAST HE WANTS TO SHOW ALL HIS FRIENDS. WHAT'S **WRONG** WITH THIS PICTURE?

●●OOO Gallop G5
100%
Nermal
Shared Just Now
Shared with Everyone
HOME SWEET HOME 2709 MAPLE STREET

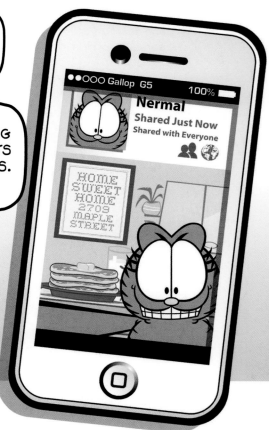

**1. Nermal's Breakfast Selfie**

A. It shows pancakes instead of waffles.

B. It shows Nermal's address on the cross stitch on the wall.

C. It doesn't show if Nermal likes hash browns.

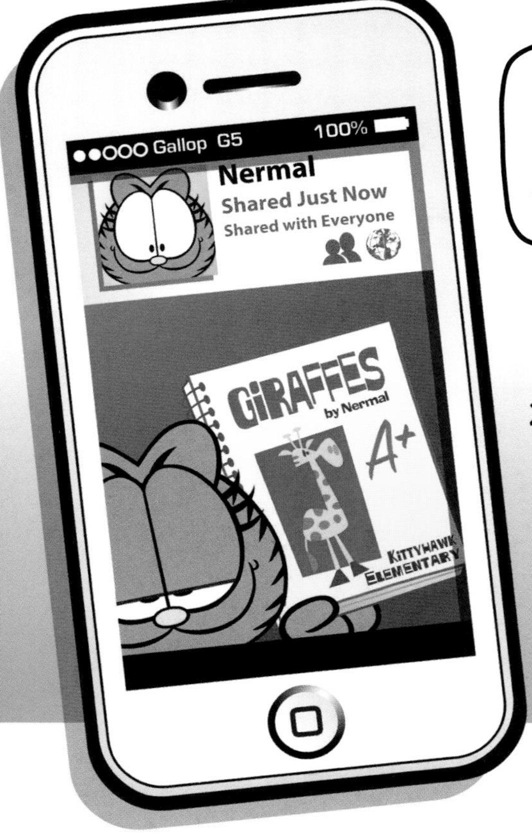
●●○○○ Gallop G5
100%
Nermal
Shared Just Now
Shared with Everyone
GIRAFFES
by Nermal
A+
KITTYHAWK ELEMENTARY

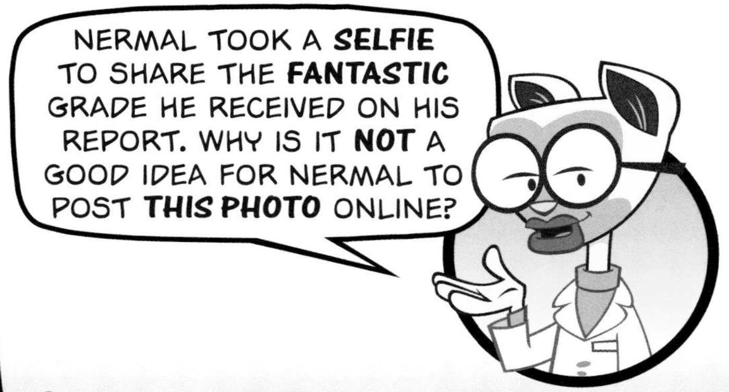
NERMAL TOOK A **SELFIE** TO SHARE THE **FANTASTIC** GRADE HE RECEIVED ON HIS REPORT. WHY IS IT **NOT** A GOOD IDEA FOR NERMAL TO POST **THIS PHOTO** ONLINE?

2. **Nermal's Giraffe Report Selfie**

    A. Nermal really doesn't like giraffes because they are so tall.

    B. You can see Nermal's name and the name of his school on the report.

    C. Nermal should only have gotten a B-plus on his report.

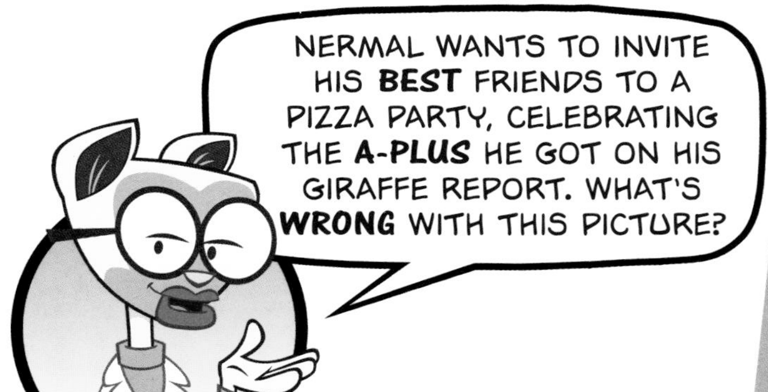
NERMAL WANTS TO INVITE HIS **BEST** FRIENDS TO A PIZZA PARTY, CELEBRATING THE **A-PLUS** HE GOT ON HIS GIRAFFE REPORT. WHAT'S **WRONG** WITH THIS PICTURE?

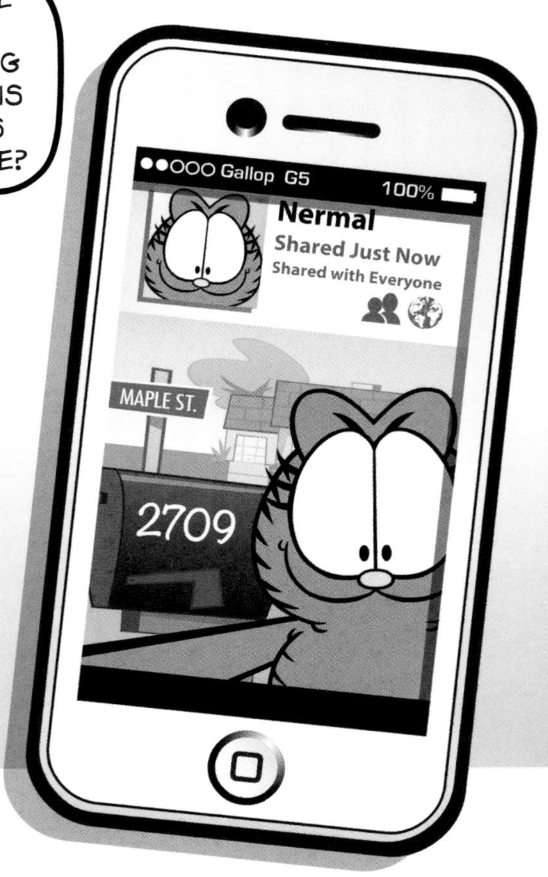
●●○○○ Gallop G5
100%
Nermal
Shared Just Now
Shared with Everyone
MAPLE ST.
2709

3. **Nermal's Pizza Party Selfie**

    A. You can see Nermal's address number on the mailbox and what street he is on in the background.

    B. You can't see all the pizza.

    C. Nermal is smiling too big.

NOW THAT YOU KNOW WHAT'S SAFE AND WHAT'S NOT, LET'S BUILD A SAFE PROFILE PAGE.

Remember, a safe profile page doesn't show personal information like age, gender, addresses, email address, phone number, or personal plans.

# PART 3: BUILD A SAFE AND SECURE PROFILE

IS THE INFORMATION BELOW SAFE OR NOT SAFE TO POST? WRITE YOUR ANSWERS ON A SEPARATE SHEET OF PAPER.

1. **Birthday: August 5**

2. **Birthday Year: 2010**

3. **School Name: Kittyhawk Elementary**

4. **Address: 2709 Maple Street**

5. **Email Address: nermal@catmail.cat**

6. **Phone Number: 555-1616**

7. **Password: 12345**

8. **Favorite Color: purple**

9. **Screen Name: cutest_kitten**

10. **Hobbies: TV, music, video games, Warriors of Cheese**

11. **Profile Picture: avatar of a cat**

12. **Class Field Trip Photo**

13. **Pizza Party Inviation Photo**

Class took an awesome field trip to the zoo! Here I am with a tiger!

Pizza party at my house on Maple Street!

## 14. Leaving on Vacation Photo

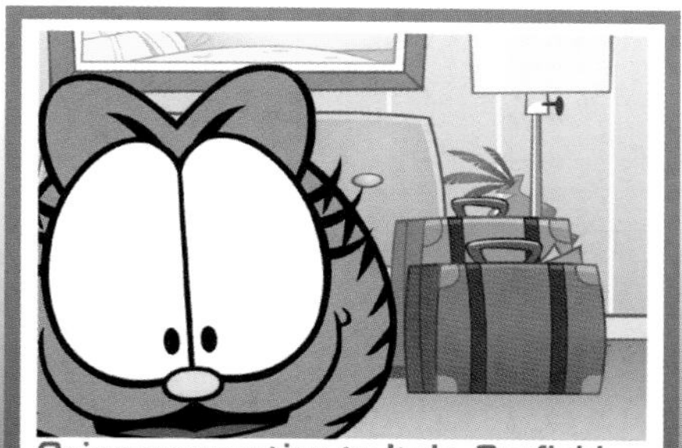

Going on vacation to Italy. Garfield wants pizza. Leaving now. See everyone next week!

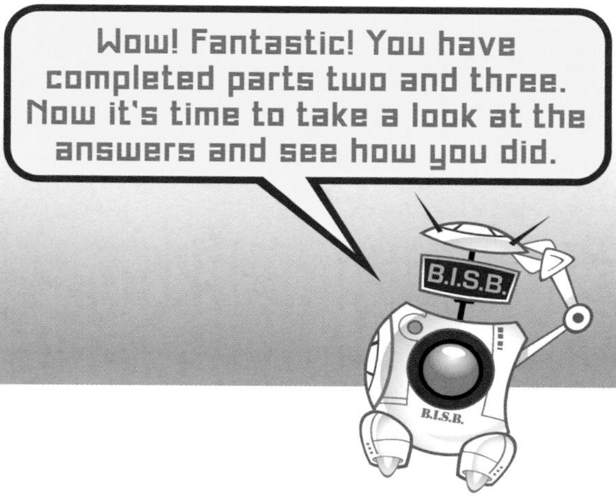
Wow! Fantastic! You have completed parts two and three. Now it's time to take a look at the answers and see how you did.
B.I.S.B.
B.I.S.B.

# PART 2: WHAT'S WRONG WITH THIS PICTURE ANSWERS

BELOW ARE THE CORRECT ANSWERS FOR EACH PHOTO.

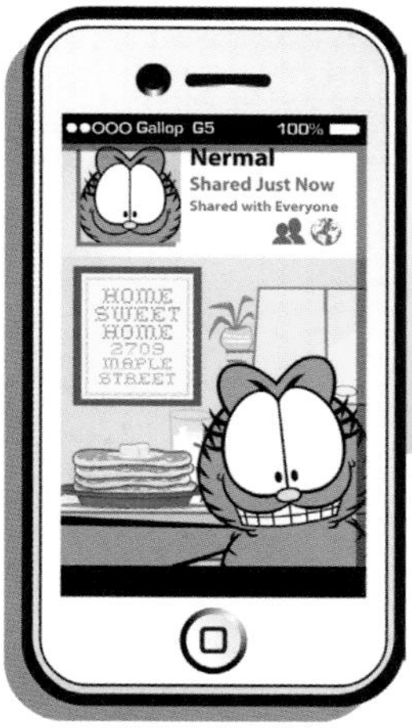
●●OOO Gallop G5 100%
Nermal
Shared Just Now
Shared with Everyone
HOME SWEET HOME 2709 MAPLE STREET

### 1. Breakfast Selfie

The answer is B. Always look for people and things in the background of photos that might be personal.

### 2. Giraffe Report Selfie

The answer is B. We need to be very careful and check what information might accidentally be in a photo before we post it online.

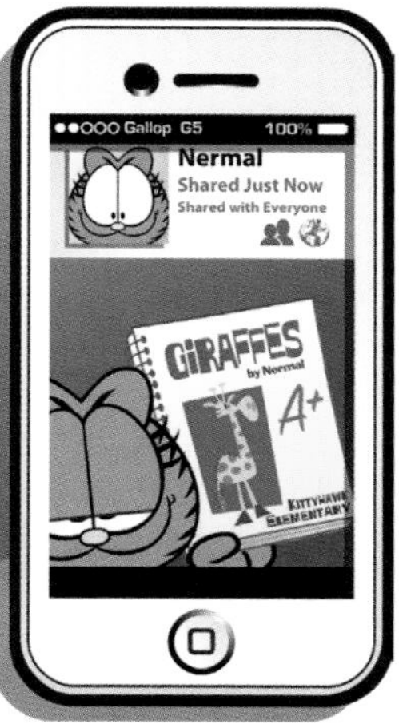
●●OOO Gallop G5 100%
Nermal
Shared Just Now
Shared with Everyone
GIRAFFES
by Nermal
A+

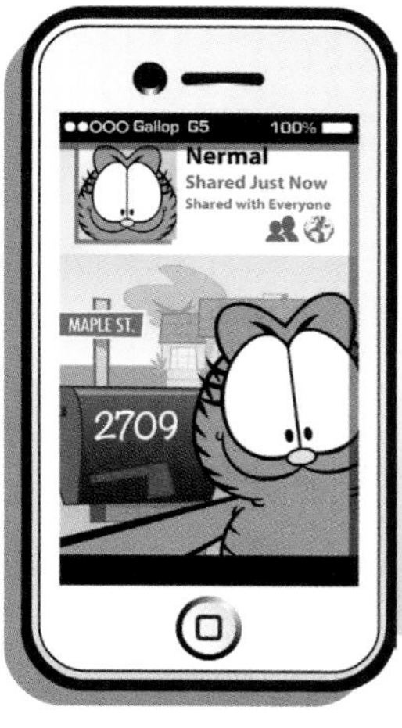
●●OOO Gallop G5 100%
Nermal
Shared Just Now
Shared with Everyone
MAPLE ST.
2709

### 3. Pizza Party Selfie

The answer is A. Be careful and never post your address or street name online where someone you don't know can see it.

# PART 3: BUILD A SAFE AND SECURE PROFILE ANSWERS

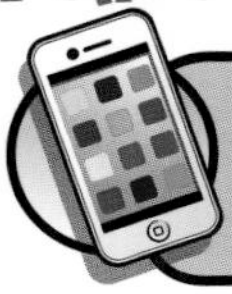

HERE'S WHAT'S SAFE AND NOT SAFE TO POST ON YOUR SOCIAL MEDIA PROFILES.

1. **Birthday: August 5**
   Safe!
2. **Birth Year: 2010**
   Not safe!
3. **School Name: Kittyhawk Elementary**
   Not safe!
4. **Address: 2709 Maple Street**
   Not safe!
5. **Email Address: nermal@catmail.cat**
   Not safe!
6. **Phone Number: 555-1616**
   Not safe!
7. **Password: 12345**
   Not safe!
8. **Favorite Color: purple**
   Safe!
9. **Screen Name: cutest_kitten**
   Safe!
10. **Hobbies: TV, music, video games, *Warriors of Cheese***
    Safe!
11. **Profile Picture: avatar of a cat**
    Safe!
12. **Class Field Trip Photo**
    Safe!
13. **Pizza Party Inviation Photo**
    Not safe!
14. **Leaving on Vacation Photo**
    Not safe!

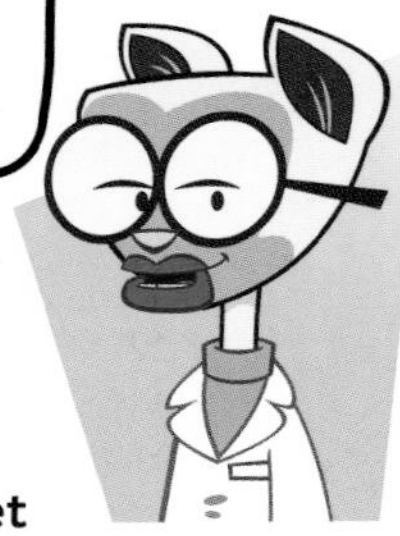
HERE ARE THE ITEMS THAT ARE **NOT SAFE** TO POST. YOU SHOULD **NEVER** PUT THEM IN YOUR PROFILE.

**Birth Year:** 2010
**Password:** 12345
**Phone Number:** 555-1616
**Address:** 2709 Maple Street
**School Name:** Kittyhawk Elementary
**Email Address:** nermal@catmail.cat

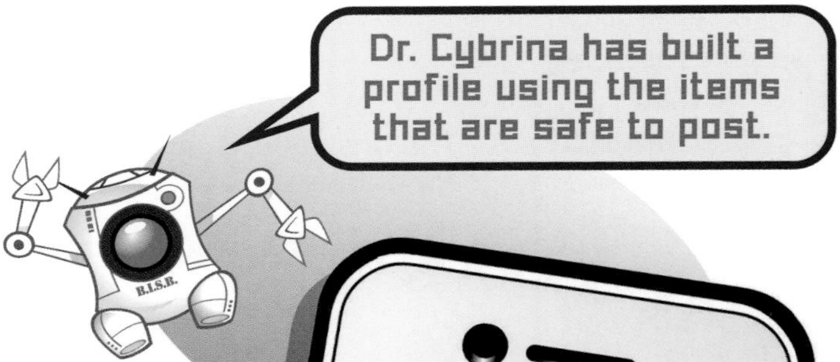
Dr. Cybrina has built a profile using the items that are safe to post.
B.I.S.B.

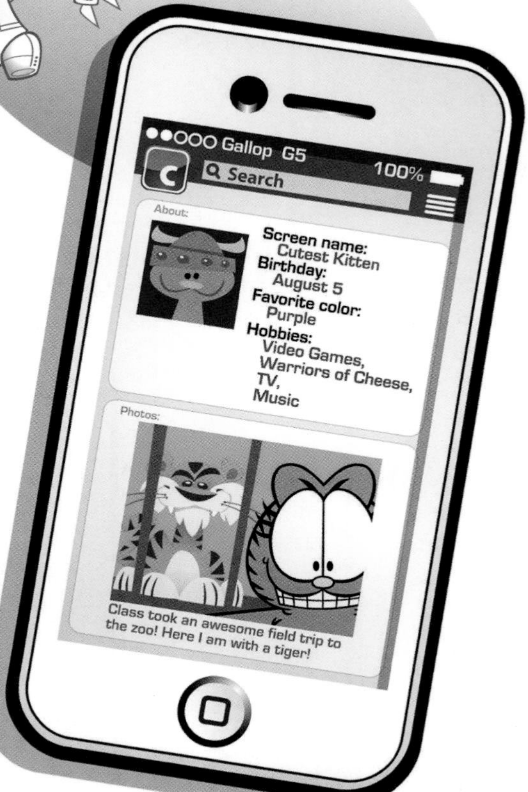
●●OOO Gallop G5
100%
Search
About:
Screen name: Cutest Kitten
Birthday: August 5
Favorite color: Purple
Hobbies: Video Games, Warriors of Cheese, TV, Music
Photos:
Class took an awesome field trip to the zoo! Here I am with a tiger!

# NOODLE ON IT!

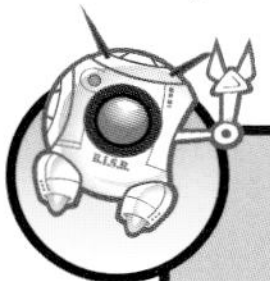

DISCUSS YOUR THOUGHTS ON THE QUESTIONS BELOW WITH A FRIEND, OR WRITE THEM ON A SEPARATE SHEET OF PAPER.

1. Have you ever felt unsafe online? Why or why not?

2. Have you ever been to a website with an age limit (minimum age requirement)? Why do you think some websites have age limits?

3. Why is it important to keep passwords private?

4. How do privacy settings help keep you safe?

5. What should you do if a stranger talks to you in real life? What about online?

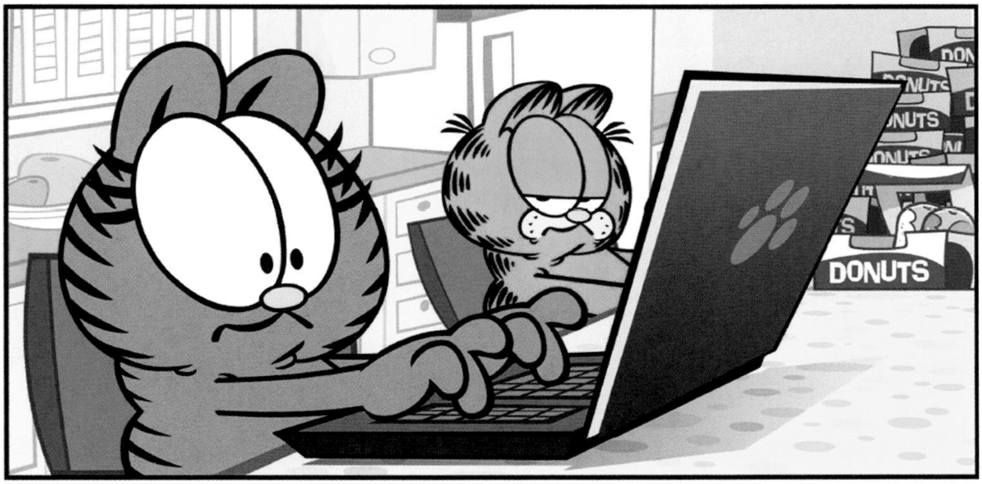
DONUTS

# INTERNET SAFETY TOOLBOX

1. **Keep personal information private, and do not share it online or in-game.**

2. **If something makes you feel uncomfortable, log off and tell an adult.**

3. **Think before you click or send. Pause before you post.**

4. **Create strong, unique passwords, and never share them.**

5. **Get permission before tagging and posting pictures of other people.**

6. Report cyberbullying immediately.

7. Never meet an online-only friend without talking to a parent or guardian.

8. Follow age rules for social media sites and games.

9. Build safe profile pages, and make sure that your settings are set to private.

10. Remember that online friends are not the same as real friends.

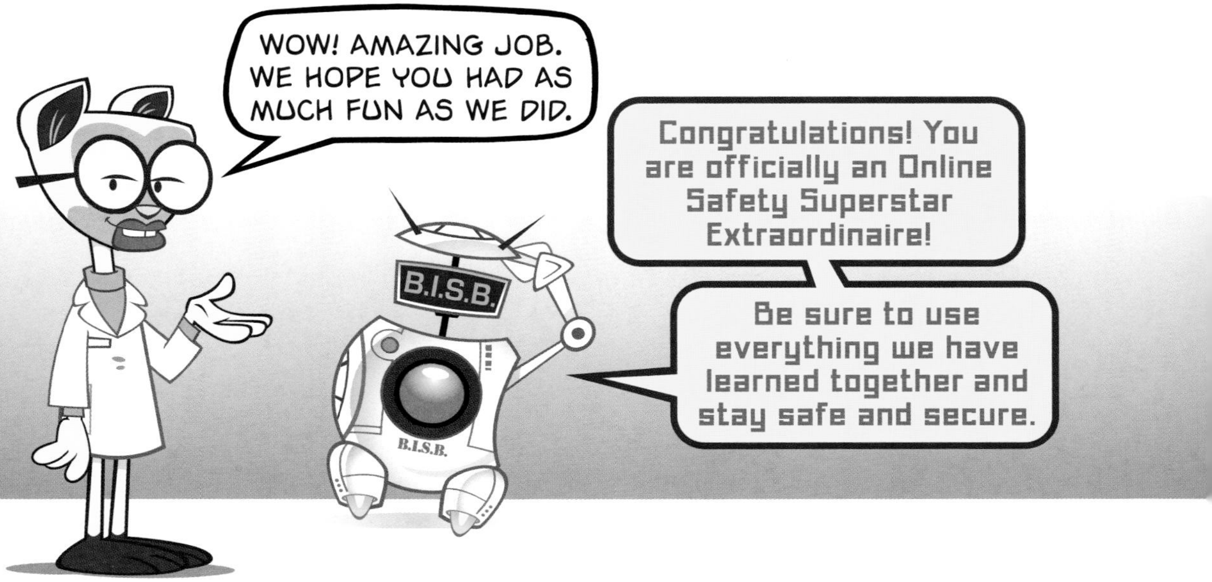
WOW! AMAZING JOB. WE HOPE YOU HAD AS MUCH FUN AS WE DID.
Congratulations! You are officially an Online Safety Superstar Extraordinaire!
Be sure to use everything we have learned together and stay safe and secure.
B.I.S.B.
B.I.S.B.

# GLOSSARY

**information systems:** systems that interpret and organize information

**online:** connected to a computer or the internet

**personal information:** information that can help to identify a particular person

**post:** to share content online

**profile:** an online location, often on social media, where information about a particular person is displayed

**social media:** forms of electronic communication through which users create online communities for sharing information, ideas, personal messages, and other content

**status:** a post on social media that indicates a user's current situation, state of mind, or opinion about something

# FURTHER INFORMATION

Anton, Carrie. *Digital World: How to Connect, Share, Play, and Keep Yourself Safe*. Middleton, WI: American Girl, 2017.

Being Safe on the Internet
https://kidshelpline.com.au/kids/issues/being-safe-internet

5 Internet Safety Tips for Kids
https://www.commonsensemedia.org/videos/5-internet-safety-tips-for-kids

Hubbard, Ben. *My Digital Safety and Security*. Minneapolis: Lerner Publications, 2019.

Lyons, Heather, and Elizabeth Tweedale. *Online Safety for Coders*. Minneapolis: Lerner Publications, 2017.

Secure Password Tips from ConnectSafely.org
http://www.safekids.com/tips-for-strong-secure-passwords/

Explore more about Cyber Safety at www.IAmCyberSafe.org

# INDEX